the
BICYCLE
SPY

the BICYCLE SPY

YONA ZELDIS MCDONOUGH

SCHOLASTIC PRESS / NEW YORK

Library of Congress Cataloging-in-Publication Data

Names: McDonough, Yona Zeldis, author.
Title: The bicycle spy / Yona Zeldis McDonough.
Description: First edition. | New York : Scholastic Press, 2016. | Summary: Twelve-year-old Marcel loves riding his bicycle, and dreams of competing in the Tour de France, but it is 1942 and German soldiers are everywhere, stopping him as he delivers bread from his parents' bakery around Aucoin—then one day he discovers that it is not just bread he is delivering, and suddenly he finds himself in position of dangerous secrets about his parents and his new friend from Paris, Delphine. | Includes bibliographical references.
Identifiers: LCCN 2016013790 | ISBN 9780545850957
Subjects: LCSH: World War, 1939-1945—Underground movements—France—Juvenile fiction. | Secrecy—Juvenile fiction. | Families—France—Juvenile fiction. | Jews—France—History—20th century—Juvenile fiction. | Cycling—Juvenile fiction. | Adventure stories. | War stories. | France—History—German occupation, 1940-1945—Juvenile fiction. | CYAC: World War, 1939-1945—Underground movements—France—Fiction. | Secrets—Fiction. | Family life—France—Fiction. | Jews—France—Fiction. | Bicycles and bicycling—Fiction. | Adventure and adventurers—Fiction. | France—History—German occupation, 1940-1945—Fiction. | GSAFD: Adventure fiction.
Classification: LCC PZ7.M15655 Bi 2016 | DDC 813.54 [Fic]—dc23 LC record available at https://lccn.loc.gov/2016013790

10 9 8 7 6 5 4 3 2 1   16 17 18 19 20

Printed in the U.S.A. 23
First edition, September 2016
Book design by Ellen Duda

For Ethan Winogrand, super-cyclist and stellar friend.

Special thanks to Judith Ehrlich and Matthew Ramsey for their invaluable assistance with the historical portions of this story, and to Becky Shapiro, a marvelous editor brimming with intelligence, enthusiasm, and energy.

the BICYCLE SPY

ONE

A gust of wind cut across Marcel's face as he cycled furiously down the street. He was riding as fast as he could, and he pushed even harder on the pedals of his trusty blue bike, but the bumpy cobblestone streets of Aucoin were not exactly made for speed. Still, he had to hurry. Just a little while ago his mother had come into his tiny room, with its narrow iron-framed bed, desk, and old armoire crammed in the corner, demanding that he get up and run this errand for her. She said it was very important.

"Can't it wait?" he had said. "It's so cold out." It was late Sunday morning, and he and his family were back from church. He was warm and cozy under a small blanket, reading an out-of-date magazine about French-born René Vietto, the second-place winner of the 1939 Tour de France.

"No," she said. "It can't. You have to bring this loaf of bread to Madame Trottier right now." Her tone was unusually stern.

So with a big sigh, Marcel set aside the magazine, ran his fingers through his mop of curly hair, straightened his tortoiseshell glasses on his nose, and reached for his jacket. He'd have to finish the article later.

Ever since Marcel had gone with his cousins and his father to see the Tour three years ago, he'd been practically obsessed with the big bicycle race and was looking forward to seeing it again. Riders from all over the world participated in the grueling competition, which was broken up into stages and went on for days. But in the spring of 1940, Germany invaded France, and shortly after that, the German army marched into Paris. The Tours de France had been canceled indefinitely. Now it was 1942, and the Occupation had dragged on for two long years. Who knew how long it would last or when the race would start up again?

The bumpy cobblestones made the bike shake. But Marcel wouldn't let that stop him. He knew that in 1939, the spring classic Paris-Roubaix bicycle race included fifteen or more cobbled sections as part of the grueling 200-plus kilometer course. Some were even steep hills.

He had just rounded the corner of the street where Madame Trottier lived when suddenly a streak of orange flashed across the road. *Zut alors!* He jammed his feet on the brakes hard and swerved just in time to miss hitting a very large ginger cat. The cat looked annoyed but not especially alarmed. What a relief. He would have hated to be responsible for squashing a cat on the cobblestones. He liked cats—his parents kept a pair of tabbies in the bakery over which they lived because they were good mousers. Sometimes when his mother wasn't looking, he would feed them scraps from his plate. They would lick his fingers with their rough, pink tongues and purr almost too softly to hear.

The ginger cat padded away unharmed but a girl darted out into the street and scooped the cat up in her arms. She had blue eyes and black hair plaited into two tight braids. Under her gray coat, he could see the hem of her dress, which was also blue.

"Bad kitty!" she said. "You could have been hurt."

"Is he okay?" Marcel asked. He thought so, but he wanted to be sure.

"It's a she," said the girl. "And she's fine, thanks." Still cradling the cat in her arms, she walked away.

Marcel stood staring after her. He had never seen her before. Maybe she was new in town. She looked like she was around his age, and she was pretty—not that he cared about stuff like that. He wasn't interested in girls. He thought they were bossy and gossiped too much. Also, they cried at the least provocation. And not one of them he knew had the slightest interest in what he considered the most important thing in life: cycling.

But why was he even standing here thinking about this? He'd promised his mother he'd hurry, and if he didn't, she would be annoyed. He loved his mom, but she did have a tendency to nag—about cleaning up, washing his hair, helping out in the bakery. Moms were like that.

When he finally reached Madame Trottier's house, he'd been pedaling so hard that despite the chilly day, he was sweating. *"Merci,"* she said, taking the bread from him. "Tell your mother I appreciate it very much."

"I will," said Marcel. He pedaled home more slowly, passing the string of shops that lined the street: butcher, cheese store, greengrocer, café, and, on the corner, bakery. On the other side of the street was a store that sold clothes, another that sold hats, and a third that sold toys. That one used to be his favorite, but now that he was twelve, he was a little too old to stop in anymore. There was also a tailor, a tiny shop that sold used books, and the town's old church, St. Vincent de Paul. He passed a few other people on bicycles as well. Bicycles were just a part of life here, and a good way to get around quickly. People young and old rode them almost everywhere.

The only thing that was unfamiliar in all this was the presence of the soldiers.

When the Germans had invaded France, they swarmed all over Paris and lots of other cities in the north. Marcel had seen the headlines in the newspapers and heard about it on the radio that Papa kept on a table in the front room. Aucoin, however, had been in the Free Zone since the invasion in 1940. That meant it was not occupied by Germans and they had not seen many soldiers here.

But in the last two weeks, that had all changed. On November 11, the Germans invaded the Free Zone, too, and now soldiers from France and even Germany had started to appear in the town square or at the market. He also noticed more gendarmes—police—patrolling the town.

The French soldiers wore belted olive green jackets and helmets. In other circumstances, he might have admired them. But given the presence of the Germans and the gendarmes, they made his little village seem like a strange and scary place. A lot of other people thought so, too, and quietly cursed the soldiers when they were not in earshot. People said that they were working hand in hand with the Germans and called them *collabos*, which was short for *collaborators*. Whatever they were called, Marcel feared and distrusted them. He wished they would all go away.

He slowed when he got to the bakery. His mother was outside, scanning the street for him. "Did you deliver the bread?"

"Yes, and Madame Trottier said to say thank you."

Only then did her expression soften. "Good. Thank you for getting it to her."

"I'm going to keep on riding for a while," he said. His mother nodded and went back into the bakery. She'd seemed so anxious lately, more so than usual. He wondered what was wrong, but when he'd asked, she'd said she was fine.

The bicycle bumped along until Marcel reached the end of the cobblestones; then he was able to pick up speed. Soon he was outside the town, pedaling faster and faster still. The houses rushed by, and the trees arched overhead, only a few dried leaves left on their tall branches. What if one day he could actually ride in the Tour de France? He'd be speeding along, just like this. As he rode, the red-roofed houses gave way to farms and pastures in which he saw horses, cows, sheep, and pigs. For a few seconds, he imagined the road lined not with animals but with crowds of spectators cheering him on as he flew along to victory.

Then he had to slow down for a gaggle of geese crossing the road, their noisy honks echoing in his ears as he passed. That ended his dreams of the Tour de France, at least for now. After a while, he grew hot and tired, so he let the bike slow to a stop and hopped off, flopping down in the dry grass. He would rest here a few minutes before heading home.

Marcel was small for his age and not the best cyclist, either. And he wore glasses. He didn't like being the smallest kid in class, the one who got picked on and teased. He couldn't do anything about growing taller or needing glasses—those things were beyond his control. But he could get stronger and faster. He *could*. That was why he'd vowed to try to ride every day, to build up his speed, his endurance, and his strength. Then the other kids would think twice about teasing him.

And that was what the Tour de France riders did. He'd been reading all about them. Most recently, the entire racecourse was 4,224 kilometers! You had to work up to a distance like that. Of course, the race was divided into stages of a certain number of kilometers each day, to make it possible to finish. There were eighteen stages in all. He also learned that the cyclists had developed special strategies, like eating certain foods and taking vitamins, all in an effort to improve their performances.

Marcel reached for his canteen, took a long drink, and climbed back onto the bike. He still felt bitter about missing what was now three years of the race; it was another reason to resent the Germans. His parents shared his resentment. They detested the Occupation, which had brought the soldiers here. It also brought rationing and shortages of food and gas. And his parents especially detested Adolf Hitler, the leader of the German people and the man responsible for the invasion and the war. But what could they do about it? Not a whole lot.

As Marcel headed back toward town, he came to a small bridge where a French soldier stood patrolling. Under his helmet, his expression was stern. The gun slung over his shoulder looked big and heavy. Marcel slowed down the way he'd been taught.

The soldier stepped out into the road and raised his hand. Marcel came to a full stop and waited while the soldier walked over and slowly looked him up and down. After a few seconds, he waved his hand, indicating Marcel could continue on his way. It was only when

Marcel had gone a little distance away that he realized he'd been holding his breath. Exhaling was a relief.

When he got back to town, he locked up his bike and went into the bakery, where he helped his mother stack the fresh loaves, swept the floor, and waited on a couple of customers before the shop closed up for lunch. Then he followed his parents upstairs to their apartment above the bakery.

"How far did you ride today?" asked his father once they were seated at the round table in the space that served as kitchen and dining room. A gas stove, sink, and small icebox lined one wall. The other held an open hutch where all their dishes were stored.

"About three kilometers," Marcel said. His father was interested in cycling and the Tour de France, too, and they liked talking about it. If France had not been occupied by the Germans, they would have gone to see this year's Tour de France together.

Marcel took a bite of his food. Last night, his mother had made a cassoulet—a stew of sausage, beans, and bacon. With all the food shortages and rationing in town, he didn't know how she'd managed to get the ingredients. But there wasn't all that much left today, and there was no bread. All the loaves from the bakery had been sold, forcing her to close early, and they had even gone through the stale loaves his mother saved to toast.

"And did you run into any soldiers?" his mother asked.

"Just one." Marcel ate eagerly. Not only was he hungry, he also hoped that if he ate more, he would grow taller. "Over by the bridge."

He caught the look his parents exchanged. "Was he French? Did he stop you?" his father asked.

"Yes, but then he let me go ahead."

"That's the second time now," his mother said. "Or is it the third?"

"I don't know," Marcel said. "Does it matter?"

There was a weighted silence during which the clink of the cutlery could be heard. Finally, his father said, "After lunch, I'd like you to deliver something to Marie Pierre and Benoit." The question about the guard was left unanswered.

"All right." Marie Pierre was his father's sister and

Benoit was her husband. They lived in a town that was a few kilometers away, and Marcel often brought them bread or pastries. He did wonder why his father hadn't asked him to do it earlier, when he'd gone on the errand for his mother. But this time, he did not protest.

When lunch was over, Marcel went back outside to get his bicycle.

"These are the two loaves of bread for your aunt and uncle," said his father, handing him a parcel wrapped in white cloth.

That was another strange thing. His mother had said there was no bread for lunch. Why didn't she serve one of these loaves? His aunt and uncle had no children and they could have easily done with just one loaf.

". . . and this is for the soldiers, in case you get stopped again," his father was saying.

"For the soldiers? Why?" Marcel asked. The package, wrapped in a red-and-white-checked dish towel, contained *pain d'épice*—gingerbread. He recognized the smell.

"It doesn't hurt to be polite," his father said. "And if you give them some cake, they might be less likely to bother you."

Marcel put both parcels in the basket of his bike. He was just about to leave when his mother came outside. The worried look was on her face again. "Don't give them the bread," she said.

"Why not?"

"They'll like the cake better," she said sharply.

He looked at his mother in surprise. What was wrong with her these days? Whatever it was, she wasn't telling.

Marcel swung his leg over the slightly beat-up bike. How he wished he had a brand-new racing bicycle, a Peugeot or a Gitane, like the Tour de France riders used. On his bedroom wall was a big poster of Victor Cosson, the third-place winner from 1938. Marcel wanted this poster because unlike the first- and second-place winners, Cosson was French. Cosson stood holding a sleek bicycle with curved silver handles. Maybe one day Marcel would have a bike like that. Maybe one day he'd even be able to enter the race . . .

Pedaling along the cobblestones, he once again reached the edge of town. He traveled in the same direction he had this morning, only when he came to the bridge, he took a right turn, not a left. As he approached, Marcel saw the soldier he had seen earlier in the day.

"*Arrêtez!*" the soldier called out. *Stop right here.* Marcel slowed his bicycle down and stopped in front of the soldier.

"I saw you before." The man had a different kind of accent than Marcel was accustomed to hearing. Maybe he came from somewhere near the French-German border. "What are you doing here?"

"I'm on my way to visit my aunt and uncle. To bring them some bread." His heart banged hard in his chest, but he tried to look nonchalant as he gestured to the white parcel.

"And what's that?" The soldier pointed to the red-and-white-checked parcel.

"*Pain d'épice.*" He lifted it out of the basket and peeled back the towel. The *pain d'èpice*, just baked that morning and smelling of cinnamon, ginger, and cloves, was very tempting. Marcel's mouth watered, but he remembered what his father had said, and held the cake up. "Here, take it. It's really good."

The soldier looked down suspiciously, but he broke

off a piece of the moist, spicy cake and ate it. Though he did not actually smile, his expression softened.

"You can go." He took another, larger piece and put it in his mouth.

Marcel got back on his bicycle and sped along as fast as he could, away from the bridge. As he pedaled, he felt himself calming down, but his stomach rumbled and grumbled. There had been no bread at lunch and he was still hungry. But the loaves of bread were still inside the basket . . . and his mother had only said *not* to give the bread to the soldiers; she didn't say *he* couldn't have a piece. He brought the bicycle to a stop, hopped off, and untied the white cloth.

Inside, the two round loaves looked fresh and delicious. The dark, chewy peasant breads were one of the specialties of the bakery. Marcel couldn't help himself. He had to have a big piece right now. Aunt Marie Pierre wouldn't mind. She always fussed over him when he went to visit.

Marcel sat down by the side of the road and, using the little penknife his father had given him for his last birthday, he began to cut through the bread. He ate the first piece quickly and was still hungry, so he tried to cut another piece. But this time, he was having trouble—the knife wasn't cutting. It seemed to be caught on something. He peered closely at the bread and wriggled the knife around. It looked like it was stuck on a piece of paper, tightly folded and wadded up. What was paper doing in there?

Marcel extracted it and unfolded it. It was a note, and he recognized his father's bold, quick handwriting on the page.

> The St. Sulpice Bridge has gotten very crowded with visitors from all over. Need to change plans for our picnic and find another spot.

Marcel read this once, twice, and then a third time. Picnics, bridges . . . what could it mean? The Saint Sulpice bridge was where he'd been stopped by the soldier. Could the message have something to do with that? But even if that were so, why hide a message about a picnic in a loaf of bread? Unless . . . maybe it was a *code* of some kind. He read it yet again. It *did* seem like a coded message.

Marcel pondered this. Who used codes? Secret groups who didn't want their communications to be easily understood. The Resistance, the French freedom fighters secretly pledged to resist the Germans, was such a group. He knew about them from kids at school and from conversations he'd heard among the grown-ups. He'd seen some of the leaflets, too, passed swiftly and quietly from hand to hand. Could his *parents* have something to do with all that? Suddenly, he wasn't hungry anymore.

The Germans had invaded the Free Zone about two weeks ago. Marcel's father had sent him to his aunt's with bread several times since then. He'd never thought anything of it. He'd been delivering bread for them since he was eight or nine. But in the past, he had only gone once a month or so. Going multiple times in only two weeks was way more than usual.

The trips he had made recently must have been about more than just delivering bread or pastries. Much more. He must have been carrying notes that were part of an effort to undermine the Germans! Maybe there had been a note in the bread he'd brought to Madame Trottier this morning. And maybe this explained his mother's anxious looks and her sharp voice.

Even though he was sitting down, Marcel's heart was beating very fast and his cheeks felt uncomfortably hot. He tried to put the pieces together in a way that added up to a different answer, but he could not. His father had written this strange note and, without telling him it was inside the loaf of bread, given it to him to deliver to his aunt or his uncle. The delivery had seemed urgent, too. There was only one explanation that made sense: Marcel's father—and no doubt his mother, too—were full-fledged members of the French Resistance.

TWO

The rest of the ride was a blur. To think that his parents were secretly working against the Germans! They must be braver than he had thought! But if they were caught . . . he could not even let himself imagine it. As he pedaled furiously, adrenaline making him fly, his mind jumped back and forth between pride and terror. In the end, pride won out. His father and mother were doing the right thing. The noble, courageous, and yes, even heroic thing. And so were his aunt and uncle. He would not say a word about what he knew, but he would keep making the trips whenever his father or mother asked. That way, it was like he was part of the Resistance, too.

Just before he reached the town, he suddenly remembered the bread with the note had been cut open and partially eaten. How would he conceal the note now? It was essential that he deliver it—he knew that. But he did not want to reveal that he was aware of what was going on. If he did, he was pretty sure his father would not let him make the trips anymore.

He got off the bike and paced around it a couple of times. *Think!* he commanded himself. *Think hard.* He dug his hands into the pockets of his jacket, hoping something he found inside would inspire him. There was only the penknife, a few marbles, a ten-centimes coin, and a book of matches. How could any of these things help? Wait—he had an idea. But could he make it work?

First he took the partially eaten loaf out of the parcel. He had to get rid of it, so he ate another chunk, then crumbled the rest into tiny pieces that he scattered in the woods. He'd been taught not to waste food but he told himself it wasn't really being wasted. There were so many birds that would swoop down and make off with the crumbs.

When that was done, he looked at the remaining loaf of bread. His aunt and uncle would be expecting to find the note inside it. How could he get it in there?

This was the second part of his idea. It was kind of crazy, but it was all he could come up with on the spot.

Using his penknife again, he made a small, careful slit in the bottom of the loaf and slid the refolded note inside. Then he used the matches to scorch the bread around where he had cut it. After a few minutes, the bottom of the bread turned black, and the slit he made was fully concealed. Now the loaf just looked like it had been in the oven too long. He rewrapped it in the cloth and pedaled the rest of the way, until he reached the cottage of his aunt and uncle.

"Bonjour," said Marie Pierre, wiping her hands on her apron as she came out to greet him. She kissed him lightly on both cheeks and ruffled his already messy hair. "I think you grew."

"I wish." Marcel stood as straight as he could in an effort to look taller.

"No, really, you did." She smiled and then turned as her husband came out of the house.

Uncle Benoit shook his hand and then asked, "What did you bring us today, Marcel?"

Marcel couldn't face his uncle as he handed him the

parcel, so he looked down and studied the pebbles on the ground.

Uncle Benoit took the bread. "Just one loaf?"

"Just one." Marcel nearly choked on the words.

But then his uncle said, "Fine. We'll have it tomorrow morning."

Marcel nodded, relieved that he would not have to see his uncle open the package of bread. If he did, the burned bottom might arouse his curiosity and lead to more questions.

His aunt wanted him to come inside for a while but Marcel was anxious to go home. Fortunately, he had a ready excuse. "I have a lot of homework," he said. "I should be getting back."

"Of course you should," Uncle Benoit said. "School is very important. Are you studying world history?"

"Yes," Marcel said.

"Good. Every boy should know something about history. What about current events?"

"Not so much."

"He doesn't need to do that in school," said Marie Pierre. "All he has to do is open the newspaper or turn on the radio. You can't get away from the current scene, can you?"

"No, I suppose not," said Uncle Benoit. His deep sigh made Marcel feel afraid, especially when he thought about the note his uncle would soon find.

After more kisses and a hug from Aunt Marie Pierre, Marcel got back on his bike. He was not lying about his schoolwork and he really did want to get home so he'd be able to finish it. His teacher, Mademoiselle Babineaux, was pretty nice, but she was also strict. She wouldn't like it if he showed up with an incomplete assignment.

Soon he was back at the bridge, and there was the soldier to whom he'd given the *pain d'épice*. The soldier saw him, too, but instead of calling out for Marcel to stop, he just raised his hand in a sort of greeting. Marcel rode slowly by, in case the soldier changed his mind. But he did not. His father had been right—offering a sweet treat had definitely changed the soldier's attitude.

When he got home, his father was in the bakery and his mother was upstairs, preparing dinner. But when the meal was ready and on the table, Marcel didn't want it. He'd already eaten that bread on the ride to his aunt and uncle's house. And anyway, his stomach twisted with what he now knew about his parents.

"You're not eating," his mother observed.

"It's just that I'm thinking about school tomorrow."

"Is there a problem?" asked his mother. "Have you finished your homework? You don't want to leave it all to the last minute."

Marcel tried not to show his annoyance. She *always* said that. "Yes," he said. "It's all done. That's not it."

"Then what?" his father asked.

Marcel hesitated. He wanted to say something about the note he had found. But to put it into words made it all the more real. And all the more frightening.

"It's nothing," he said. "May I be excused?"

Back in his room, he arranged his notebooks, pencils, pens, and other supplies in a neat pile on his desk, just like he did every night before school. Maybe if he acted like everything was normal it would be. But deep inside, Marcel knew that things were not normal in Aucoin, and were not likely to be for some time.

THREE

Early the next morning, Marcel pedaled off to the three-story brick schoolhouse that was three streets down from the church. He had gone here since he was a little kid, and this was where he would stay until he graduated next year. He knew the long corridors with their highly waxed floors and the classrooms with their rows of slanted wooden desks, chalkboards, and big windows as well as he knew the rooms in his own apartment.

The day was unexpectedly warm, and he stopped to unbutton his jacket. Under it he had on a white shirt tucked into dark blue knee pants, and he wore matching dark blue knee socks. Then he slung his satchel back over his shoulder and checked that his tin lunch box was in the bicycle's basket.

On his way, he spotted a couple of older boys on a corner. One called out to him, "Hey, shrimp!"

"Are you getting shorter?" yelled the other. Then they both began to laugh as they walked away.

Marcel felt his cheeks getting hot but he said nothing. When he heard his name called out, he tensed. Were they coming back to torment him some more?

But no. He turned to see his friends Guillaume and Arnaud waving him over. He got off the bike and locked it on the rack before going to join them.

"*Ça va?*" said Guillaume. *How's it going?*

"*Ça va,*" Marcel said. *It's going fine.* Much as he wanted to, he was not telling anyone, not even his good friends, about his parents and the Resistance. It was too dangerous to talk about. Resistance members who were caught were interrogated and sent to prison. Or worse—they might even be shot.

"I saw you riding the other day. How's your speed?" Arnaud asked.

"Getting better every day," Marcel said. "How about you?"

Arnaud liked racing, too, and sometimes they raced each other. Arnaud was taller, with longer legs, so he often won. But Marcel was scrappy and fearless on the bike. He'd keep on riding through conditions—mud, rocks, ditches, ice—that would make many boys turn back.

"How about a race after school today?" asked Arnaud. "We'll go to the road behind St. Vincent de Paul that leads out of town."

"You're on!" Marcel hoisted his satchel over his shoulder and headed into the classroom. "We'll see who's the best rider."

Once Marcel got settled at his desk, he felt less anxious. At least there were no soldiers in school. All that was taking place somewhere else, somewhere outside these walls. Here in the schoolroom, with neat rows of wooden desks, its big map of France in the back of the room, and its black chalkboard in the front, everything was familiar and safe. The faces around him were faces he'd known for years. Even Mademoiselle Babineaux was someone he knew. She'd been coming to the bakery every Saturday for as long as he could remember.

But as he looked around the room, he saw that there was one girl he did not know—though he recognized her. It was the girl he'd seen in the street, the one whose cat he'd nearly run over. Today she wore a red-and-black-plaid dress with a white collar, and her braids were neat and shiny.

"I heard she's from up north somewhere. Maybe Paris," whispered Guillaume, who sat beside him and must have seen him staring. "Her family just moved here."

Ever since the Occupation, their little town had started attracting newcomers. Some settled in, while others were just passing through. Which would it be for the new girl?

"What's her name?" Marcel asked.

"Delphine something or other," said Guillaume.

"And why did her family come now, in the middle of the term?"

Guillaume shrugged. "How would I know? Anyway, why are you so interested?"

"No special reason," said Marcel. He hoped he wasn't turning red.

"Boys!" said Mademoiselle Babineaux. "Stop your chattering and pay attention."

"Yes, mademoiselle," said Marcel. He said nothing more to Guillaume, but all morning long, he continued to watch the new girl. When Mademoiselle Babineaux taught the geometry lesson, Delphine's hand shot up every time; every time she got the answer right. When she wrote at the blackboard, her penmanship was perfect. During the literature portion of the lessons, she recited a poem by Pierre de Ronsard from memory. *"Très bien,"* purred Mademoiselle Babineaux.

The only place she seemed to falter was when Sister Bernadette came in to instruct them in religion. The new girl did not raise her hand, and when she was called on, she gave the wrong answer. Some of the other kids snickered softly. At first Marcel was glad to find out that she wasn't so perfect, but when he saw her go pink with embarrassment, he felt sorry for her more than anything else. He knew what it was like to be teased and laughed at, too.

At recess, he saw her talking to some of the other girls, including Paulette, who thought she was the smartest girl in the school, if not the whole world. But why was he thinking about her so much?

He deliberately ignored the new girl and sat down to a game of chess with Arnaud, who had brought a small board from home. Chess was very popular and they did this almost every day at recess. Marcel wasn't such a good player but he was trying to get better. His father had even gotten him a book that outlined all kinds of strategies for winning.

Once Arnaud set up the board and arranged the pieces, the game began. Arnaud was a good player, moving his rook, his knight, and even his queen with a boldness that Marcel lacked. Still, he studied the board carefully and tried to ignore the comments from some of the other boys as they gathered around to watch.

"Quiet!" ordered Arnaud. "If you guys can't shut up, you'll have to leave. Chess is serious business. You have to concentrate, not blab." The boys quieted down and the game continued.

Last time they played, Arnaud had won. Today, Marcel was determined to be the winner. But Arnaud's aggressive style undermined his confidence, and he watched, miserably, as Arnaud swept piece after piece off the board. Finally, Arnaud proclaimed, "Checkmate!" and the game was over. "Loser, loser!" chanted Arnaud as he put the pieces away in a drawstring cloth bag.

Marcel said nothing. They were good friends but that didn't stop them from competing with each other about pretty much everything. Marcel knew that if he'd won, he probably would have taunted Arnaud in exactly the same way.

Later, when the bell rang for lunch, Marcel decided to avoid Arnaud entirely. He didn't want to hear him crow about his victory all through the break. So instead, he found himself focusing again on Delphine, this time as she stood in the lunchroom, looking around uncertainly. None of the girls she had been talking to at recess seemed to have invited her to sit down, so she took a seat at a table by herself. He followed her. "Can I sit here?" he asked.

She looked up, her blue eyes interested and curious. "You're the boy with the bike. You almost ran over my cat."

"I didn't mean to," said Marcel. "Anyway, you told me the cat was fine."

"She is."

"I'm Marcel Christophe," he said as he sat down.

"Delphine Gilette," she answered. She reached into a

cloth sack and pulled out a sliced baguette layered with cheese.

"You're new here." He opened his lunch box. His meal was very similar to hers: baguette with ham, and a few cornichons—tiny, tangy pickles.

"We just moved here," she said.

"From where?" he asked.

"Oh, different places . . ." She seemed reluctant to talk about where she had lived.

"Someone said you came from Paris," Marcel ventured.

"Well, we did, but that was before—" She stopped herself.

"I've never been to Paris," said Marcel. "What's it like?"

Her blue eyes brightened. "Paris is the most wonder-ful city in the world," she said. "We have everything: the Louvre, the Jardin du Luxembourg, the Métro—"

Marcel knew she was talking about a famous museum, a public garden, and a subway system. But he'd never seen any of those places except in photographs.

"I guess you were sorry to leave," Marcel said as he crunched on a tasty cornichon. It had been hard to get these pickles lately. His mother must have stashed a jar away.

Delphine gave him a shrewd look and took a bite of her baguette. "Yes and no. I love Paris. It's my home. But since the Germans came, it didn't feel like it was mine anymore."

"I know what you mean," he said. Then he thought that Aucoin couldn't feel much like home to Delphine, either. It must have been hard to move away from everything you knew and leave all your friends behind. "Hey, do you want a cornichon?" he offered.

She looked hesitant but finally took one. "Thanks," she said. "I haven't had one of these in a while."

The bell rang, signaling the end of lunch. Marcel picked up his lunch box.

"Maybe you can come to my house one day after school," he said. He actually kind of liked her. She seemed so different from the other girls he knew. "We live above the bakery. My parents own it. I could help you with religion—" Her eyes narrowed until he added, "And you could help me with everything else!"

She laughed. "Maybe I will. You seem pretty good at religion. Or maybe we can ride our bicycles together some time."

"Do you have a bicycle?" asked Marcel. A girl who liked to ride a bike? Now, that was *really* interesting.

"It's my brother's. My mother doesn't like me to use it." She made a face. "But he's away at school in London, so what's the harm? Anyway, she doesn't know, but I even rode it to school today." Flipping her braids over her shoulders, she walked back to the classroom.

Marcel followed close behind. When he sat down at his desk, he found a folded note on the seat. He opened it and read it quickly.

> Don't forget about the bicycle race today! I hope you don't chicken out because I'm going to win! I beat you at chess and I'll beat you in a race, too!

Marcel smiled. Arnaud liked to boast. Well, let him. Marcel wasn't scared. He could beat Arnaud; he *would* beat him! He could almost hear his classmates' cheers as he sailed across the finish line. Arnaud may have been the better chess player but Marcel was pretty sure he was the better cyclist.

Thinking about the race made the afternoon drag. They had a science lesson and then music. Usually, music class concluded with the whole class singing "La Marseillaise," which was the French national anthem. In the last two weeks, though, they had not sung it. Maybe the Occupation had something to do with that.

But then the dismissal bell rang and Marcel's focus instantly turned back to the race. He hastily stuffed his books into his satchel, picked up his empty lunch box, and went outside with all the other kids. Delphine was nowhere to be seen. But that didn't matter—he went over to his bicycle and quickly pedaled to the appointed place near the church.

Arnaud was already there, hands steadying his black bicycle. Guillaume and a bunch of other kids had turned up, too, laughing and jostling one another. The afternoon had warmed up even more. Marcel took off his jacket, wadded it up, and stuffed it into his bag.

"Are you ready?" called Arnaud.

"I'm ready," Marcel called back. He handed his bag and lunch box to Guillaume and maneuvered his bicycle into position. But before they could start, Marcel heard his name. He turned, and there was Delphine, riding up on a handsome red bike and ringing its silver bell. That bike was really something, and the bell was great, too—shiny, with a forceful sound when she pressed it. Marcel wished he had a bell like that on his bike!

"I want to race, too," she said.

Arnaud looked at Marcel; Marcel shrugged. "I don't know," he said. "We've never raced a girl before, have we?" Arnaud shook his head.

"What difference does my being a girl make?" said Delphine. "I've got a bike. I'm taller than Marcel, but not as tall as Arnaud. It seems fair to me."

"She's right," said Guillaume, and then several kids chimed in, "Let her race! Let her race!"

"Okay," Arnaud said finally. "Come over here and get in line with us. We'll start at the church and then keep going until we come to the big oak tree, way down the road. Whoever gets there first is the winner."

"Sounds good." Delphine positioned herself between Marcel and Arnaud and gave her braids what Marcel now realized was her trademark flip.

He didn't know how he felt about racing a girl. Delphine had already demonstrated what a good student she was—now was she trying to prove that she was the best cyclist? Not if Marcel had anything to say about it! He hunkered down over the handlebars.

Standing by the finish line was a boy named Alain. He was in charge. "On your mark," he called, "get set . . . Go!"

Marcel took off, speeding down the road like he was being pursued by demons. He kept his gaze steady on the road ahead of him and tried to block out the knowledge that Arnaud had pulled ahead and Delphine was gaining on him. Marcel pedaled faster and faster, until he'd caught up to Arnaud and then passed him. Yes! He was doing it, he was going to beat them and—

All of a sudden, Delphine shot ahead like a blazing red rocket, leaving both Marcel and Arnaud behind. The crowd of kids chanted her name, "Delphine! Delphine!" Marcel kept pedaling, but he'd lost his focus and his edge. As his glasses slipped down the bridge of his nose, Arnaud whizzed past him. But Delphine was still ahead of them both. Marcel's eyes clouded with tears as she reached the oak tree and turned around to face the group triumphantly.

"The winner!" called out Alain. He pressed down on Delphine's bell a few times, and then he yanked her arm up in the air, a gesture of victory. Arnaud was there seconds later, and then Marcel, in third and last place.

Panting with exertion, he angrily swiped at his eyes and pushed the glasses back into place. It took several seconds for his breathing to go back to normal. Delphine had come out of nowhere to win the race. Who even knew a girl could go that fast, riding her brother's bike besides? As Marcel stood watching her, so many things were swirling around inside him. Shame, anger, and disappointment. But also admiration. And respect.

FOUR

That night, it took Marcel the longest time to fall asleep. He tossed and turned, kicking at the covers, yanking at the sheets, and even punching his pillow to fluff it up. In his mind, he kept reliving the humiliation of the race. Beaten—and by a girl. When he finally did fall asleep, he dreamed that he was riding in the Tour de France, only he was the very last cyclist in the race, straggling behind everyone else. The crowds that lined the side of the road jeered and tossed rotten vegetables at him as he passed. It was a relief to wake up.

At breakfast, he could hardly stay awake. Twice his mother asked him if he was all right. He told her he was fine, though he wished he could say he was sick and crawl back into bed. But he knew if he did that, the other kids would think he was ashamed of being a loser—so ashamed that he had to stay home. No, as tired as he was, he had to go to school today.

So after he ate, he picked up his satchel and headed down the road on his bicycle. When he reached the school building, he saw Delphine. He didn't feel tired anymore as she came right up to him. "I have something to show you," she said. "I know you're going to like it."

"What is it?" he asked, curious. He was glad she did not make fun of him about losing to her.

"It's a surprise," she said. "Wait until recess."

All morning he wondered what it might be, and when recess came, Marcel was the first one out the door. Delphine followed close behind. He noticed she was lugging something in her satchel. While the other kids ran around, chasing each other and shouting, they walked to a shady spot at the far end of the schoolyard. There were a couple of big, flat rocks over there and Delphine sat down on one of them, then pulled something from her bag. *"Voilà,"* she said. *Look.*

It was a big leather-bound scrapbook. Marcel opened it to look inside. It was full of pictures of all the winners of the Tour de France! Some, like Antonin Magne and

Ottavio Bottecchia, had actually won *twice*. Now, that was really something to be proud of. Along with the photographs, there were articles cut out from newspapers and magazines, maps, and postcards that showed the cyclists' smiling faces peering out. There was even a bit of yellow fabric glued to one of the pages.

"What's this?" Marcel touched the faded snippet.

"A piece of a jersey that belonged to Roger Lapébie," she said.

"He won in 1937," said Marcel.

"Right," said Delphine. "My grandfather knew someone who knew him."

"Was all this stuff your grandfather's?"

"He started making the scrapbook. Then my father added to it. And I'm adding even more." She reached over to flip the pages ahead. There, close to the end of the book, were more-recent pictures, which Marcel recognized.

Delphine continued. "My grandpa and my dad are both big Tour de France fans. Not my brother, though. He doesn't care about cycling at all. Isn't that funny? I'm a girl, but I love it." She let go of the pages and nudged the book back in Marcel's direction.

"This is some collection you've got here." Marcel was impressed. He began to leaf through the book more carefully. Soon some of the other kids, tired from running around, came over to join them.

"Hey, can I see?" asked Arnaud.

"Sure." Delphine moved aside so he could have a look. Guillaume and some of the others crowded in, too, all jostling to find a good spot.

"Where did this come from?" Arnaud asked. When Delphine explained, he added, "I bet it's worth a lot of money."

"It could be," Delphine said.

"So where did you get it? Is your family rich or something? Like all those Jews who are wrecking the country?" said Arnaud.

Marcel looked over at Delphine, who had not answered. Two big pink splotches appeared on her cheeks and it seemed that her lips were trembling. Why was she so upset? Arnaud could be kind of a jerk, but basically he was all right. And plenty of people supported the new government headed by Maréchal Pétain and said bad things about Jews: that they had too much money, were taking over the country, were foreigners, and were not true Frenchmen. Marcel's parents never talked like this and so neither did Marcel. He didn't even know any Jews. But he wasn't really bothered by these comments, either. Yet Delphine was—why?

Arnaud didn't seem to expect a reply. And he clearly didn't have any idea he'd upset Delphine. He was looking at the scrapbook, pointing, exclaiming, and laughing. So was everyone else. Was Marcel the only one who noticed her reaction?

He moved over to her. "He's an idiot," he said softly. "Just ignore him."

Delphine nodded, though she said nothing. But she seemed to calm down.

Then the bell rang. Recess was over. Delphine put the scrapbook back in her bag, and everyone headed to the open doors and filed back into the classroom. But Marcel kept thinking about the comment and Delphine's reaction to it. There was some mystery about her—something that made her seem different than the other girls he knew. But he couldn't have said what it was.

He mentioned the exchange to his parents later that evening. "Why do you think she got so upset when Arnaud said that about her family being rich?"

"I'm not sure," Papa said.

"What did you say her name was?" Maman asked.

"Delphine," said Marcel. He noticed his parents exchanging a look.

"Delphine what?" asked Maman.

"Gilette," answered Marcel.

"And she just moved into town? Did she say why?"

"No, she didn't," Marcel said. "Anyway, why are you so interested? She's just a girl at school."

"No special reason," Maman said. She suddenly seemed very absorbed by the sewing in her lap, and her fingers moved deftly as she worked.

But Marcel was not fooled. He'd said pretty much the same thing to Guillaume when Guillaume had wanted to know why *he* seemed so interested in Delphine. He hadn't been telling the truth then and he suspected his mother was not telling the truth now. But before he could say any more about it, she looked up from the shirt whose buttons she was replacing.

"Your room is a mess," she said. "Didn't I ask you to straighten it up earlier?"

He sighed. "You did."

"And yet it still isn't done."

"No . . . ," he said, knowing what was coming next.

"Then would you please go do it now?"

With a big sigh, he got up from his chair. "What difference does it make anyway? Who even cares if my room is messy?" But he said it softly, so she wouldn't hear. And then realizing that any argument would be futile, he went off to do what she had asked. It was only when he'd picked up all the clothes from the floor and stuffed them, unfolded, into his armoire, pulled the blankets up in an effort to make the bed, and gathered all the papers and books and tucked them behind a chair that he thought again about his mother's interest in Delphine. She'd said there was no special reason for it. So why didn't he believe her?

FIVE

When Marcel got home from school the next day, his mother asked him to take another loaf of bread to his aunt and uncle. Marcel was not in the mood to do the errand. He was tired and wanted to read the new comic book he had traded with a kid in school, not hop on his bike. But the look on his mother's face made him realize it was pointless to protest, and so he waited while she wrapped the loaf in a clean white dish towel. Then she handed him another parcel wrapped the same way. It had a familiar and delicious aroma. *"Pain d'épice?"* he asked.

"Yes. In case you get stopped."

He took the packages and put them in the basket of his bicycle, which he had left in front of the bakery that morning—it had been raining and he had not wanted to ride in the rain. The sky was clear now, yet he still didn't want to ride: Though he hated to admit it, even to himself, he was a little bit afraid. Before, he'd thought he was just delivering bread and cakes. Now he knew better.

There was probably a message inside the loaf. What if a soldier or a gendarme took that loaf and found it? But then Marcel looked at the other parcel, the freshly baked *pain d'épice*. He would offer that to anyone who stopped him. That's why his mother had given it to him—to keep him safe. And she was asking him to do this for a good reason. At least he thought it was for a good reason. They were working against the Germans, who had invaded their country. That was a noble thing to do, right? The thought made him feel a little better.

"Don't stay long at your aunt's house," she said. "I want you to come right back."

"I will, Maman." Marcel got on his bike and pedaled down the streets until he had left town and was on the open road. The trees overhead had lost all their leaves now, and only the bare branches remained. He saw a rabbit dart across the road and scurry off into the high grass. Usually, he liked this ride. He'd fantasize about the Tour de France and pretend he was riding in it. These empty roads would be filled with adoring fans. He could almost hear them as he rode . . .

Today it was different, though. He could not be lulled into the familiar fantasy, and he kept looking down at the basket with its two covered loaves. When he came to the bridge, he recognized that soldier he'd seen before, and he slowed down. The soldier recognized him, too. Marcel came to a stop. He was scared. What if he wanted the bread today?

"Do you have cake?" the soldier asked. Marcel nodded. With slightly shaking hands, he handed the soldier the *pain d'épice*. The soldier inclined his head and took the package. And when he pulled back the cloth to reveal the aromatic loaf inside, his mouth turned up in a small smile. "Go," he told Marcel in his strangely accented French. Marcel didn't waste any time getting back on the bike and speeding away.

He got to his aunt's house about twenty minutes later and gave her the loaf of bread. Was there a note inside? He had not dared to check.

Before he turned around to leave, his aunt handed him a worn shawl. "Please bring this to your mother."

That was strange. His mother already had a nice shawl. Why was his aunt sending another?

"I'll give it to her." As he put the shawl in his basket, he realized it was made of two different kinds of material that had been sewn together. One side was bluish gray and the other, light brown. There was room in between the two sides. And when he was far enough from his aunt's house, he stopped to examine it more closely. There was something *in* there—something that felt like a piece of folded paper. Instantly, he knew: It was a note that his aunt and uncle were sending to his parents.

Marcel sped back home as fast as he could. The guard at the bridge waved him through so he didn't even have to stop. He saw his mother standing out in the street, like she was waiting for him to get back. Why? Did she think he wouldn't make it?

"You got here quickly," she said. "Did anyone stop you at the bridge?"

"Only when I was on my way there, but I gave him the *pain d'épice* again and he didn't stop me on the way back. He even smiled, sort of."

"I'll have to keep baking the cake," his mother said. "I just hope I can get the ingredients. There are always shortages at the market."

"Aunt Marie Pierre sent this to you." He gave his mother the shawl with the note sewn inside it. It took every bit of self-discipline he had not to blurt out, *I know what you and Papa are doing.* But he didn't. If he told, they might not let him deliver the loaves anymore. And scared as he was, Marcel wanted to keep carrying the messages. It made him feel brave, strong, and important. His mother just thanked him and draped the shawl over her arm, like it was nothing special.

The next day at school, Mademoiselle Babineaux asked Delphine to sit in the front row, at the desk directly opposite hers. This was a place of honor in the classroom and although Marcel had a seat in the first row, he'd never been asked to sit in that special desk. Paulette, the girl who had occupied the place before, did not seem happy about giving it up, and everyone was talking about it at recess. Marcel did not join the cluster of kids who were in the yard, but he stood close enough so he could hear. He didn't see Delphine anywhere.

"The new girl thinks she's better than everyone," Paulette said. "That seat was mine. I'm the best one in the class. Just look at my marks."

"I'm not so sure," said Guillaume. "She seems pretty smart to me."

"She's not smart. She's pushy, that's all. She thinks she can waltz in here from Paris or wherever and just take over."

"Sounds like you're jealous," said Guillaume.

"Who, me?" Paulette was indignant. "Why would I be jealous of her? I just don't like her, that's all."

Paulette had a high, whiny voice. Marcel turned away and went back into the classroom by himself. There was Delphine, sitting at her desk. "How come you're not outside?" he asked. "Recess isn't over for another fifteen minutes."

"I don't feel like it," she said. She kept her head down

and did not look at him. Maybe she'd heard something, he thought. Maybe she *knew*. He went back outside to play with the other kids but his heart wasn't in it. He was glad when recess was over.

Later, when school was dismissed, he saw Delphine walking home alone. He wanted to go talk to her, but he thought about what Paulette had said and he was afraid. If he got *too* friendly with her, the other kids might start teasing him for that, too. There was already enough that he was picked on for. Still, she knew so much about cycling, and she was a really good rider. And he even felt a little sorry for her.

Marcel waited until Delphine got to the end of the street and turned the corner. Then he rode his bike through the tiny alley beside Madame Girard's flower shop so he could meet up with her on the other side, out of sight of his classmates. What he did was his own business. No one had to find out if they became friends, did they? And he was going to make sure that they didn't.

She looked surprised to see him waiting—but not unhappy. "What are you doing here?" she asked.

"Looking for you," he said. "I wanted to see that scrapbook again."

"All right," she said. "But we can't go to my house."

"Why not?"

"It's because of my mother. She's not well and she doesn't like me to have anyone over." She seemed nervous when she said this. Like she was lying. But why would she lie about that?

"We can go somewhere else," he said. "I'll show you a good place, and you can go home and get the scrapbook."

Marcel walked his bike as they fell into step together. Soon they came to an abandoned barn that was near the edge of the town. He pushed open the door and they stepped inside.

"Is this your secret hideout?" She walked around slowly, looking at the empty stalls and piles of pale, dried-out hay.

"Sort of," said Marcel. He and Arnaud used to come here but Arnaud complained that it smelled, so they had stopped. It would be a safe place to meet Delphine. "If you want to get the scrapbook, I can wait here."

"I'll go as fast as I can," she said. "I'll even run."

Marcel was about to offer her his bike, but then he thought better of it. Arnaud or one of the other kids might recognize it if they saw her on it. So he said nothing, and she left. He sat down in the straw and started to get comfortable.

It seemed she was back in no time.

"How'd you get back here so fast?"

"I took my brother's bike!" she said, and wheeled the red bicycle inside. A shaft of light from a high window shone brightly on the silver bell. "And here's the scrapbook." She set it down and they began to look at it together. The smiling winners in the pictures looked so happy and so proud. Marcel could imagine how they must have felt. "Do you think the race will ever start up again?" he asked.

"If the war ever ends," Delphine said. "It's been going on for a while now."

"Too long," said Marcel.

"Way too long," she agreed.

They continued to turn the pages and chat until the light from the window faded and the barn grew dim.

"I guess we should go now." Marcel stood and brushed the hay from the back of his pants.

"Au revoir," she said. *Good-bye.* "Meet here tomorrow?" she asked as she hopped on her red bike.

He nodded. *"Au revoir."* He got on his bike, too, and swiftly pedaled home.

SIX

For the next four school days, Marcel and Delphine met after school at the barn. He would bring something left over from the bakery, like a bit of stale bread or a couple of rolls, and she'd bring a nearly empty jar of jam or honey, and they would have a snack. They did their schoolwork together, and Delphine showed him tips on how to fix his bike or adjust the seat and handlebars so he could get better speed and control. She had a worn leather pouch that held a couple of wrenches, a screwdriver, and a few other tools useful for fixing bikes. He couldn't believe how much she knew about bicycles— more than he did, or any of his friends.

"How did you learn all this?"

"My dad fixes bikes for a hobby. He even built one himself. He tried to show my brother how, but my brother didn't care. So he showed me. See, this is where you want to have your seat—you were riding too low."

They never actually said it out loud, but she seemed to understand that if they were going to be friends, they shouldn't advertise it. Other than Paulette, the kids in school seemed to accept her and didn't bother her too much about having been chosen to sit in the seat of honor.

On the fifth day, though, they decided to ride together, out beyond the edges of town where it was unlikely they would be seen. It was cold, but Marcel warmed up when he rode. Faster and faster he pumped, but he still couldn't catch up to Delphine. Finally, in a furious burst, he pulled ahead until they were riding side by side. In seconds, they reached an abandoned stone well, their agreed-upon finish line.

He stopped, hopped off the bike, and sank down into the tall grass that was now white and dead. She did the same. He turned and propped himself on one arm so he could get a better look at her. Even though she won most of their races, she never made fun of him.

"I just wish I could be as fast as you are." He sighed deeply.

"You've got to learn to pace yourself better," she said. "And I think you're not hunched down enough over the handlebars. Here, let me show you." She got up and reached for her bike to demonstrate. She was a good teacher, patient and encouraging. But there was no time to try out her suggestions in another race, at least not today. They said *au revoir* and went their separate ways.

The sky was darkening when Marcel pedaled along the cobblestone street to his house. He'd stayed out too late. His mother would be mad. "There you are," she said when he came up the stairs. "Wash up—dinner is just about ready."

Marcel went to the sink and washed his hands and his face, too, and then sat down to join his parents for the evening meal. The familiar blue-and-white bowls held soup. It was thin and kind of tasteless, but he didn't want to complain about it. More food shortages, he guessed.

"How's school?" his father asked.

"Everything's fine."

"And your friend Delphine? Everything all right there?"

"How did you know we were friends?" Marcel asked. He thought he was doing a good job of keeping that secret.

But his father just turned on the radio and was soon immersed in listening to the broadcast from Radio Paris.

The next Monday at school, Marcel and his classmates were busy working on their compositions when a noise made him look up. Two German officers had come into the room, their shiny black boots heavy on the floorboards, their armbands with the thick black swastikas threatening. Even more threatening were the enormous black guns they carried, so casually looped over their shoulders, like satchels. Marcel was pretty sure they were from the Gestapo, the German secret police.

It was bad enough seeing the soldiers in town, as he had a few times. But there had never been any Gestapo officers in school. Seeing them here made it feel like they had invaded his classroom—and his world. What would they do if they knew about his parents being in the Resistance? Drag them from the bakery? Force them to answer questions? *Shoot* them? An icy terror washed over him as these terrible scenes unfolded in his imagination.

One of the officers said something to Mademoiselle Babineaux and then gestured for her to follow him out into the hall to talk. Marcel noticed that she took her big book with her, the one that had all the names of the students written in it.

While they were gone, the other officer glanced around. It seemed to Marcel that his gaze came to rest right on Delphine. Why? What reason did the soldier have to look at her? Though maybe he had imagined it. He was so anxious about the possibility that his parents could be discovered that he was jittery about everything.

He was not alone in feeling like this. Usually, when the teacher was out of the room, some of the kids would start misbehaving. Things got thrown, or names were called. Not today. Everyone remained in his or her seat, cowed and quiet. Mademoiselle Babineaux and the soldier came back into the room. She seemed frightened. Her face was pale and she did not look at the class. She nodded vigorously as the soldier who had remained in the room said something in a low voice, but she did not look at him, either. Finally, when the two soldiers left and she closed the door behind them, there was a feeling of relief in the air, as if the whole class had just exhaled in unison.

"Please continue with your compositions," Mademoiselle Babineaux said. For a few minutes, everyone returned to his or her writing, and the only sound in the room was the scratch, scratch, scratch of pens on paper. Then the bell rang. Recess! Marcel was the first one out of his seat. The classroom felt oppressive and even frightening, like a jail cell. He couldn't wait to get out.

In the schoolyard, everyone was talking excitedly about the officers.

"Did you see their guns?" asked Guillaume.

"How could you miss them?" asked Arnaud. "It's not like they hid them or anything."

Marcel shuddered, remembering. He listened to the others talk for a few minutes more, then he wandered away. Delphine was nowhere around. Where had she gone? He went back inside and looked in a couple of empty classrooms. She was not in either of them.

After a minute, his classmates began straggling in, Guillaume first, and then Arnaud, laughing and jostling each other. Mademoiselle Babineaux went straight to her desk and began rearranging the papers on its surface as if it were the most important task on earth.

Then Delphine came in. She looked pale and shaken. Her braids, usually so neat and tight, were messy, and he had the sudden thought that she'd been crying. But she would not catch his eye and kept her head bent over her schoolwork. He wouldn't be able to talk to her until after school, so he reluctantly pulled his gaze away and tried to focus on his composition.

When school let out, he rode over to the barn and carefully concealed his bike inside. A little while later, Delphine showed up in her worn gray coat, a black beret on her head. When she saw him, she actually jumped back, a look of sheer terror on her still-ashen face.

"Hey, it's just me," he said. "And you know I'm not going to hurt you."

"No, but they are!" she burst out.

"What are you talking about?" he asked.

"The Gestapo! Those men who came into our classroom!"

"I know," he said sympathetically. "They're pretty scary."

"I hate them!" she cried passionately. "Hate them!"

"I hate them, too," Marcel said more quietly, thinking of his parents and the grave danger they faced from such men. "More than you could ever know."

"What do you mean?" Her blue eyes blazed. "What are you saying?"

Marcel was taken aback by her response. "I just meant . . . that is . . . you see . . ." Should he tell her? Yes or no? He felt ripped apart inside.

"Are you . . . ?" Delphine began.

"No, it's my parents." It was a relief to say those words, to tell *someone*. "They're in the Resistance. They don't know that I know. But I found out. I've been delivering notes in the bread, the bread from the bakery and—"

"The Resistance!" She pulled off her beret and tossed it to the floor. "I thought you were going to tell me something else."

"What else would it be?" He was truly perplexed by how upset she seemed.

There was a long silence during which she would not look at him but stared down at the floor. Finally, she picked up a bit of hay and began twirling it with her fingers. She raised her eyes to his. "That they're Jewish," she said in a low voice. "That you all are."

"Jewish?" Whatever was she talking about? Why would she even think that?

"Yes, Jewish. Like me." Her eyes, now glassy with tears, locked on his. "And you have to promise—no, swear!—not to tell. Ever!"

"Okay, okay!" Marcel nodded. "Jewish!" He repeated. He was stunned. He didn't think he'd met anyone Jewish before. Everyone he knew was Catholic and went to the church of St. Vincent de Paul on Sundays and saints' days, or holidays like Easter and Christmas. "But that can't be! I mean, how—"

"My father is a lawyer. Or he was, until he wasn't allowed to practice law anymore. But he knew people who could get us out. He was able to pay them for their help."

"Is that why—?"

"We left Paris and have been moving around? Yes." She had dropped the bit of hay and began pulling on the tips of her braids, her nervous fingers tug, tug, tugging. "Things in Paris were terrible. We had to wear armbands with yellow stars on them. They said *Juif* in the center. I was so frightened when I wore that armband in public. And ashamed, too—like being a Jew was a bad thing."

"That sounds awful," said Marcel.

"It was. And it only got worse. In the summer, thousands of people were rounded up in the winter sports center at the edge of the city. We heard it was horrible. No food, no water, people all crammed together. They were . . . deported."

"What does that mean?" asked Marcel.

"Taken somewhere far away. We're not sure where.

Drancy, maybe." She must have read his puzzled look. "That's an internment camp. There are others, too. In Germany," she explained.

"But not your family," he said.

"No. My father was able to get us forged identity papers. Delphine Gilette is a fake name. My real name is Rachel Neumann. They got us ration cards, too, and other documents we needed. We moved around for a while, heading south, trying to get to the border. Then he found us a place to stay. Some people in the Resistance arranged it. That's why we're here."

Marcel was quiet for a moment, trying to absorb all this startling new information. Then he thought of something else. "You said you had forged papers and a fake identity. But I've never seen you in church."

"Christian doesn't have to mean Catholic," she said. "My father said we would pretend to be Protestants. He thought that would easier."

"So that's why you had such trouble when Sister Bernadette called on you that day."

She nodded. "But I've been studying," she said. "I can't afford to let her catch me again."

"You must be afraid all the time. What if someone finds out and tells on you?"

"It would be terrible," she said. "So when Gestapo officers came into the classroom today, I was so scared! I'd seen them in Paris. I know what they do to people like me. They round us up and they lock us up. And then they kill us."

Hearing that, Marcel felt like he'd been punched in the stomach. How could this even be possible? But somewhere inside he knew it was. He'd seen newspaper photographs of Paris in which the Nazi soldiers seemed to be everywhere. Huge banners with big black swastikas were hung from public buildings. Clusters of Nazis were all over the streets, bars, and restaurants. He also knew that the Germans despised the Jews and had passed laws against them. Jews lost their jobs and were banned from public places. So what Delphine had just told him—or should he call her Rachel?—was the logical extension of all that. No wonder her family was desperate to get away. They thought they would be safer here in the country. Only today that hope just may have crumbled—for good.

The sky around had darkened and a few early stars could be seen. "If my parents are in the Resistance, they might be able to help you!" Marcel said. "Like the Resistance workers who helped you leave Paris. Should I ask them?"

Rachel looked uncertain, and then shook her head. "No. Don't say anything. I mean, my parents said I shouldn't tell anyone about us. And look—I've already gone and told you."

"Think about it," he said. "Maybe they could help."

"Maybe." She stood up. "I'd better get going." Her voice sounded hollow and sad. "My mom is waiting."

Marcel wished he could say something that would be of some comfort to her, something that might even help. Instead, he said the only thing he could think of, which was, "Don't worry. I'll never tell anyone your secret. Never."

"Thank you." And although she did not smile, her expression looked a little less bleak. But only a little.

SEVEN

After Delphine had left the barn, Marcel waited a few minutes and then got back on his bike. As he rode along the familiar streets toward home, his mind was racing as quickly as his feet were pedaling. So Delphine and her family were Jewish! That explained a lot of things. Things that had not quite fit together before suddenly did, like the pieces of the giant jigsaw puzzle that he and Papa had worked on together all of last summer.

There, coming down the street, he caught a glimpse of two gendarmes. It was true that they were not quite as scary as the Germans, but with the dangerous secrets he now knew, he didn't want to meet up with them.

Quickly, he turned a sharp corner and hid behind a big shrub to avoid them.

He was just in time, too, because they stopped walking, and one of them pulled out a cigarette and lit it.

Marcel stayed where he was, concealed by dead leaves and thorny branches. Remaining motionless and silent, he strained to listen to what they were saying. Much of it was uttered too softly for him to make out, though he could tell they were gossiping and complaining. A few words were clear enough to understand: Very soon, the officials were going to recheck the papers of newcomers to town, especially those who had arrived in the last eighteen months.

Marcel knew Delphine and her family had gotten to Aucoin more recently than that. And their papers were false, a fact that might be easily discovered during a routine check.

He remained where he was, choked with fear. The gendarme who had been smoking stubbed out the end of his cigarette with the heel of his boot. Then the two gendarmes walked off. When the coast was clear, Marcel sped home.

At dinner that night, he shared with his parents what he'd heard the gendarmes saying. He wished he could tell them what he now knew about Delphine. But he didn't want to break his word to her.

"That's bad." His mother put down her knife and fork. "They'll be looking for people with suspicious papers. And if they find any . . ."

"What will happen?" asked Marcel.

"They could be deported."

"Deported to where?"

There was a silence. Then his father said, "We're not really sure. But we've heard some talk about work camps . . ."

"More like prison camps," his mother said grimly.

Delphine had said internment camps. Was this the same thing? But he couldn't ask his parents—he had promised. "Work camps? Prison camps? Why would they be sending people there? What did they do?" He tried to get more information while still keeping his friend's confession a secret.

"It's not about what they did," his father said. "It's more about who they are."

"What are you talking about?" But he knew. He *knew*.

"The Germans are deporting Jews," said his mother.

"It's been happening in Germany, Poland, Lithuania . . . and it's no different here. The Nazis have their policies and the French are just going along with them," added his father.

Delphine and her family were Jewish. If they were deported, where exactly would they be deported to? And what would happen to them when they got there? Marcel had sworn not to reveal Delphine's secret to anyone, not even to his parents. But with what he found out on the way home, he knew they were more at risk than they realized. What if his parents could help her? Would it be all right to break his promise? He wished he knew.

Marcel met Delphine in the barn the next day after school. It was the first of December and had gotten too cold for a bicycle race. Instead, they played cards, using a worn deck Delphine's mother had brought from Paris. After their game, they lingered for a few minutes to talk.

"I told my parents about the Gestapo officers who came to school," she said. "That really frightened them. They said it's not safe here anymore."

"They're right. It isn't," he blurted out. "The officials are going to recheck the papers of anyone new to the town! I overheard it last night." He hadn't been able to find the right moment to tell her before now.

Delphine's face went white, and she took a deep, shaky breath.

"Thank you for telling me. I already heard my dad telling my mom that we have to escape—now I know that he's right."

"Escape? Where?" The hair on the back of Marcel's neck began to prickle and he knew it wasn't just from the crisp, cold air.

"I'm not sure," she said, tugging on the tip of a braid. In the distance, the church bell tolled the hour and Delphine stood up. "I've got to go." She brushed off the back of her coat. "I'll see you tomorrow. I guess."

Marcel rode home. That brisk wind had turned sharper and colder, and he shivered under his jacket. He was glad to see the lights of his own kitchen window. After dinner, he went into his room and closed the door. He was still undecided about whether to reveal

Delphine's secret to his parents. She was afraid, he knew. But what if they could help?

A knock on the door startled him. "Come in," he said.

"I need you to take a loaf of bread to someone tomorrow," said his father. "But since it's getting dark earlier these days, I was wondering if you could do it before you went to school."

"Do I have to?" He didn't want to get up that early. He might even be late getting to class. Usually, his parents did not like him to do anything that would interfere with school. *Education comes first*, Maman was fond of saying.

"Yes, you do," said his father.

So the message inside the loaf of bread must be really important. Urgent, even. He thought of everything that was happening now: the Gestapo, Delphine and her family. "All right, Papa," he said. "I'll go first thing in the morning."

"Thank you," his father said. "I won't be here when you leave but Maman will have the bread ready for you."

"Where will you be?"

"I heard there might be flour available in Perpignan and I'm going to drive over to pick it up. I haven't been able to get a new bag for a couple of weeks and we're almost all out."

Marcel understood. His father needed the flour to bake the bread that was their living. And then he had another thought: If there were no loaves of bread, his parents would not have a place to stash the messages they needed to send.

That night Marcel lay awake for a long time. He was so worried about having to get up early that he was unable to drift off to sleep. It must have been close to dawn when he finally felt himself relaxing. The sky was growing lighter and he could hear the first chirps of the birds. He really should be getting up to deliver the bread soon. But he was tired. So very tired. He'd close his eyes for just a few minutes and then he'd get up and be on his way . . .

The next thing he knew, sunlight was streaming into the room. Marcel bolted straight up in the narrow bed. What time was it? He must have slept too long. Now what was going to happen? Was it too late to deliver the bread?

He grabbed his clothes as quickly as he could and went into the other room. The chairs were arranged neatly around the table, which was covered in a red-and-white-checked cloth. The familiar earthenware bowl sat in its usual spot. Beyond that were the armchairs in which his parents liked to sit after dinner and the window with its starched lace curtain. But the rooms were empty. No one was there.

Marcel clattered downstairs to the bakery. No one was down there, either. The shelves were not even half full. The door was locked and the sign saying *Fermé—Closed*—hung in the window. All of this was very strange.

Then he spied a loaf of bread wrapped in a white cloth. A small piece of paper with his name on it was pinned to the top. So that was the loaf of bread he had been meant to deliver. But where were his parents? He knew his father was picking up the flour, but shouldn't he be back by now? And what about his mother? She was always here to open up in the morning. That was one of their busiest times.

There was a clock hanging on the wall behind the cash register. It was nine thirty. So he was late for school, too. He picked up the bread and gripped it tightly in his hands. Should he pedal over with the bread, even though it was late? Or should he go to school? He'd never been so confused in his life. Or scared: Where *were* his parents? Maybe something bad had happened to them. If he knew that they were members of the Resistance, maybe someone else did, too. What if they had been betrayed and were in danger?

Then he heard a noise outside. Papa! He raced to meet him just as he was unlocking the door and walking in. What a relief to see him.

"Marcel!" His father seemed surprised to find him in the bakery. "Why aren't you at school?" Then he noticed the bread in Marcel's hands. "You didn't deliver it, did you?" he asked.

"No, Papa, I didn't and I'm really sorry! But I was so worried about waking up in time that I couldn't fall asleep for hours. Then I overslept this morning." Marcel thought he was too old for tears, but he felt like crying now. "And then when I didn't see you or Maman I got kind of scared and didn't know what to do."

"The wheel of the wagon came off and I had to stop to fix it," Papa said. "That's why it took me so long to get back." He looked around the bakery. "I don't know where your mother is," he said. "I have to find her."

"What about the bread?" Marcel asked.

His father took the loaf and stared at it for several seconds. "I'm afraid it's too late to deliver it now," he said. "You go on to school. The delivery will have to wait."

"But what about the message, Papa?" Marcel couldn't hold in the question a second longer. "Isn't that why you wanted me to deliver it? Because of the message inside?" His heart was hammering wildly as he waited for his father's reply.

"So you know," his father said. He didn't seem surprised or alarmed, only very sad. Even defeated. "Maman and I had wanted to keep it from you. How did you find out?"

Marcel told him the whole story. Papa listened

carefully, and when Marcel was finished he said, "Maman and I agonized over whether we should let you make these trips and deliver the messages. She said no at first. But in the end, we thought it was important enough to take the risk. So much is at stake—for all of us." He took a deep breath and went on. "We didn't tell you because it was safer that way. And we didn't want to frighten you. But now I see you've known for a while and made the trips anyway. You're a brave boy and I'm proud of you. Maman will be, too."

Marcel felt three inches taller—that's how proud he was. But there was still Maman to worry about. "But where is Maman?" he asked.

"I don't know," said his father grimly. "But I'm going to find her."

"What can I do? I want to help you."

"Go to school. Act like nothing's wrong."

"That's all?" Marcel asked.

"That's enough for right now," Papa said.

"All right." But then Marcel saw that his father was pulling aside the white cloth and slicing the bread lengthwise. "What are you doing now?" he asked.

"Getting rid of this." His father pulled the folded note from the center of the loaf. "It's not safe to have it anymore." Then he walked to the sink at the far end of the shop, placed the note in the basin, and pulled out a book of matches. The tiny flame flared brightly before he let it fall onto the note. In a matter of seconds, he was running the water, washing whatever was left down the drain. Then he turned back to Marcel. "Go on, now," he said. "There's nothing more either of us can do if we stay here." When Marcel still did not move, he added, "We need to pretend things are all right. That's the safest and the smartest course."

Papa was right. Marcel knew that. So, hoisting his satchel over his arm, he headed down the stairs, where his bicycle was waiting. He sped along the familiar streets that now felt strange and sinister. Soon he was at school, where he hoped he was ready for whatever the day would bring.

EIGHT

Marcel tried his hardest to concentrate on what his teacher was saying, but it wasn't easy. Several times when Mademoiselle Babineaux called on him, he could not come up with a reply, and he just sat there, as silent as a turtle. "Marcel's got his head in the clouds today," she said. Everyone laughed but he hardly even cared. All he could think about was his mother. Where had she gone? Was she all right?

Finally, it was time for recess and he burst into the yard with the other boys. The day was cold and gray but they ran around wildly anyway, glad to be released from the discipline of the classroom. Marcel joined in, running back and forth the length of the schoolyard. At least it kept his mind from dwelling on his mother.

The girls kept their distance, clustered together in a group over by the fence. Then he saw a boy named

Thierry run close to the girls and grab Delphine's black beret from her head.

"Hey!" She spun around. "Give that back!"

Thierry gave a snort of laughter and kept running. Delphine was fast, but Thierry was so big, and his legs were so long. She could not keep up with him. He ran around the schoolyard with the beret, tossing it up in the air and letting it drop. Delphine pursued him for several minutes but she abruptly stopped.

"You can keep it," she said. "I don't even want it anymore." And she turned away.

Thierry stopped, too. He dropped the beret onto the ground and then stalked off, into the school building. Marcel was torn. He knew what it was like to be bullied by Thierry. Last year the bigger boy had made his life miserable with his teasing and taunting. Once, Thierry had stuck his foot out to trip Marcel as he passed. Marcel had fallen, books scattering everywhere. Another time Thierry had cornered him in the schoolyard and wouldn't let him pass. This year, the bully had found other victims and seemed less interested in tormenting Marcel, but Marcel still kept his distance. He hated to see the bigger boy teasing Delphine, but he was afraid to confront him. Anyway, Thierry wasn't interested in bothering Delphine now. It was clear that the game was only fun if she tried to get her beret back. When she lost interest, so did he.

He watched as Delphine went over to retrieve the beret, which she did not put on but stuffed in her pocket. Recess was just about over anyway and they would all go back inside. When the bell rang, she was the first one in.

Back in the classroom, Mademoiselle Babineaux had just told them to take out their geometry books, when Mademoiselle Vernet, who worked in the school director's office, came into the classroom carrying a note. Mademoiselle Vernet stood waiting while Mademoiselle Babineaux read it. Then the teacher stood up. "I must go and speak to the director right now," she said. Her gaze moved over the rows of pupils. "Marcel," she said. "Please come up front and sit at my desk. I'm putting you in charge." Then she turned to the class. "Open your books to page thirty-six, and do all the problems on that page. I'll expect to see them done by the time I get back."

Carrying his geometry book, Marcel walked up to the front of the room. It felt strange to sit at Mademoiselle Babineaux's desk and to see the classroom from this unfamiliar vantage point. "Be good," Mademoiselle Babineaux said. "If you're not, I'll be sure to hear all about it." She nodded to Marcel and then she and Mademoiselle Vernet left the classroom.

At first, everyone did as their teacher said and started working on the problems. Marcel did the same. Most of them were pretty simple but down near the bottom of the page, the problems were more difficult and he had to work harder to figure them out.

He looked up and noticed that Thierry was not in his seat. Where had he gone? Marcel looked around anxiously. Then Thierry emerged from the coatroom. A nasty smile was painted on his face. "Look what I have!" Thierry crowed. He was waving something above his head—a satchel. Marcel had a sick feeling he knew whose it was.

"That's mine!" Delphine cried, standing up at her desk. "Give it back!"

Thierry just laughed his cruel, barking laugh and held the satchel high above his head where Delphine could not reach it. She got out of her seat and ran over to him. Vainly, she tried to retrieve her satchel. But she was too short.

The other kids remained in their seats, looking uncomfortable. No one joined in, but no one tried to stop Thierry, either.

Marcel didn't know what to do. Where was Mademoiselle Babineaux? Why was she taking so long? She had left him in charge, though. He had to do something.

"That's enough!" Marcel said sternly. He didn't know where he found the courage to say this, but once he got started, it was easier to keep going. "Put that down!"

"Like you're going to make me?" Thierry sneered. In horror, Marcel watched as Thierry dumped the contents of the satchel all over the floor. Delphine dropped to her knees and scrambled to gather books, a flowered handkerchief, pencils, a wooden ruler. He saw her hand reach out for a slim blue pen but Thierry's big foot got there first. There was an ugly crunch as he ground it under his heel.

"You'll get in trouble," Marcel continued. "Big trouble."

"He's right," Guillaume piped up. "Give it back."

"I'll give it back when I'm good and ready!"

Delphine was still awkwardly collecting her belongings and Marcel went over to help. Thierry was digging through the satchel though it appeared to be empty. Then he said, "Hey, what's this? A secret compartment? What are you hiding in here, anyway?" Thierry reached into the pocket and pulled something out. It was small and ivory colored. A card of some kind. No—a photograph. And there appeared to be some writing on the back.

"Give. Me. That," hissed Delphine.

Marcel was close enough to see Delphine go white with fear. The look on her face was so awful that it goaded him to try to grab the photograph from Thierry's big, meaty hands. But it was too late. Thierry had dropped the satchel and was studying the photograph. "That's you," he said accusingly to Delphine. She said nothing. "That's you with a boy. Is he your brother? And what's that building behind you? There's a six-pointed star on top. And the boy—he's wearing one of those stupid skullcaps!" He flipped the photo over, so Marcel could see the image of Delphine, younger but still recognizable, and her brother, standing side by side. *"Rachel and Roger Neumann, Paris, 1939,"* Thierry read. Then he raised his head in wonder. "You're a Jew," he said. And then repeated it more loudly. "A dirty, stinking Jew!"

"You don't know what you're talking about! You're crazy!" she said. Marcel looked at her with awe. There she was, caught and exposed—but she didn't cower or give up. She threw herself at him and succeeded in snatching the picture from his pudgy fingers.

"That's right," Marcel said. "Crazy! I'm telling Mademoiselle Babineaux. She'll be so mad." His mind darted back to the picture—Roger must be her older brother, the one who was in boarding school in England.

"Not when she hears what I just found out."

"You found out nothing," Marcel bluffed. "A big, fat nothing. It was just a picture. A picture you haven't even got anymore. Who's to say you're not making it all up?"

"Because I have names," Thierry said. "And names are even better than pictures."

The other kids stood silently watching as this drama played out in front of them. Just then, Mademoiselle Babineaux walked back into the classroom. She looked very displeased. "Marcel, I left you in charge. So why are you three out of your seats?" she scolded. "Everyone return to your desks immediately."

Dirty Jew, mouthed Thierry silently before heading for his desk.

"Mademoiselle Babineaux?" said Delphine hesitantly. The photograph was nowhere in evidence. She must have shoved the crumpled remains into her satchel. "I'm feeling sick. Very, very sick."

"*Je suis desolée,*" said Mademoiselle Babineaux. *I am sorry.* "Do you need to go home?"

"Yes, mademoiselle," said Delphine. "That's exactly what I need to do. Right now. May I please be excused?"

Mademoiselle Babineaux touched her hand to Delphine's forehead. "Why, you're burning up," she said. "You must have a fever. Yes, you are excused. You may get your things and go right now."

"I have my satchel," said Delphine. "I just need my coat."

"I'll get it," Marcel volunteered. He did not want her to have to walk past Thierry's desk. "Stay here."

"Thank you, Marcel," said Mademoiselle Babineaux. "That's very considerate of you to offer."

Marcel did not look in Thierry's direction as he hurried to the coatroom and got Delphine's gray coat. Back in the corridor, he handed it to her.

"You get some rest," said the teacher. *"À demain."* *See you tomorrow.*

But Marcel knew that Delphine would not be in school the next day. And when he saw Thierry mouthing the words *dirty Jew* in his direction, he also knew that if she wanted to stay safe, she would never return to school again.

NINE

Marcel was so shaken up by what had happened that he almost forgot about his mother's disappearance. And he couldn't even go home right away to find out if she had returned, because Mademoiselle Babineaux had asked him to stay after school to clean up the classroom. The janitor had been inducted into the army and there was no one left to do the job but students. So for a good thirty minutes, Marcel was busy emptying the trash, pounding the erasers until they emitted big clouds of chalk that filled the air, washing the blackboard, and sweeping the wooden floor. It seemed the work would never end. Each time he finished one task, she gave him another. Finally, though, he seemed to have finished.

"*Merci*, Marcel," she said. "You did a good job today. Thank you."

Marcel smiled. Mostly he liked Mademoiselle Babineaux. And now, if she'd only let him go home, he'd like her even better!

It was after five o' clock when he locked up his bicycle in front of the bakery. He found his father in the kitchen, awkwardly trying to prepare the evening meal. This was a bad sign—it meant Maman had not come back yet. Marcel set down his satchel and then went to the sink to wash his hands so that he could pitch in, too.

"Do you think she's all right?" he asked as they worked. He wanted to tell his father about Delphine but this did not seem like the time.

"I hope so." His father didn't meet his eyes.

"She didn't leave a note or anything?"

"No note," said Papa. "Not a word."

Dinner was soon ready and they sat down to eat. The chicken, a tough old bird to start with, was dried out and the scant bit of rice was dry, too. But Marcel didn't care because he was hungry enough to eat anything. So was Papa. Then his father put his empty plate aside and laced his fingers tightly together. "She's got to be home soon," he said, more to himself than to Marcel. "She's just got to."

Marcel did the washing up as Papa wiped down the table. At around seven o'clock, Marcel saw his father take his jacket and cap from the hook near the door. "Where are you going?" he asked. He suddenly did not want to be alone in the apartment.

"I can't just sit here and do nothing. I'm going out again. I've got to find her, or at least keep trying."

Marcel was just about to say *please let me come with you* when he heard light footsteps coming up the stairs. Then the door opened—Maman!

Marcel and his father rushed over to her. "We were so worried about you," Papa murmured. "We didn't know where you were or what happened."

"I knew you would be and I'm so sorry. But it all happened very quickly. I had to drop everything and there was no time to write a note and no way to tell you where I was, or what I was doing." She took off her coat and ran her fingers through her hair. Marcel had never seen her looking so pale and worn-out.

Papa led her to the table, where he fixed her a plate of food. Even though it wasn't very good, she wolfed it down, too. She must have been very hungry. "The police picked up Pascale Garnier this morning. She was brought in for questioning and they wouldn't let her leave for hours. Her husband was away. No one could reach him. There was no one to watch her children, so I had to go over to her house and stay with them. The baby cried all day." She sighed. "I couldn't send you a message, though. It was too dangerous."

Marcel knew Madame Garnier. She and her husband and their three little girls lived several streets away in a small stone house with a garden in front. Out back, they kept a donkey and a spotted sow. Madame Garnier was always pleasant enough when she came into the bakery to buy her breads and rolls, but she was not a close friend of the family's. So why had his mother felt the need to do this, especially when it seemed so dangerous?

As if he had read Marcel's thoughts, Papa said, "Pascale is one of us." Marcel saw the look of fear painted on his mother's face. Then Papa added, "He knows,

Simone. He told me he found one of the notes baked into the bread and he figured it out."

"You must never, *ever* tell—" Maman pushed her plate aside and stood up. She seemed very agitated.

"He understands all that," said Papa. "He says he wants to help."

Maman sat down again. "That's good," she said, more quietly now. "Very good. Because if we are going to stop these devils from taking over completely and destroying not just our country but the whole *world*, we're going to need all the help we can get."

"What happened to Pascale?" Papa asked.

"There was nothing they could prove so they finally let her go. But they wanted the names of all her friends, people she associated with. They told her they were putting her on a 'to be watched' list. I waited to leave until her husband got back. She was very shaken, let me tell you."

"So are you," Papa said.

Mama buried her face in her hands. Then she lifted it up again. "But I'm all right. All of us are. And we have to be as brave and focused as we've ever been in our lives."

Marcel sat down across from his mother. Yes, he was shaken. Frightened, too. Who wouldn't be? But his mother's courage was contagious. He felt it washing over him. Now was the time to tell his parents about Delphine's family. It was worth the risk. After what had happened at school today, he could see that they had to escape—and it needed to be as soon as possible.

"There's something I have to tell you," he began. Quickly, he filled his parents in on the situation: the visit from the Gestapo, the revelation that Delphine and her family were Jewish, the awful way she had been exposed by Thierry today. He was breaking his promise, but he had to. He *had* to! Delphine needed help and this was the only way he could give it to her.

"I thought they might be Jews," said his mother. "The fact that they moved here so suddenly, in the middle of the school year. And no one has seen very much of them. They keep to themselves."

Marcel remembered how Delphine had not been allowed to bring friends home. That must have been why.

"That boy Thierry," said Papa. "I know his parents. They support Pétain and the whole rotten Vichy government. If he tells them, it's certain that they'll inform on your friend."

"Isn't there anything we can do?" Marcel asked. "Anything at all? They're not safe in Aucoin. Not anymore."

"They're not safe anywhere in France," said Papa.

"Delphine said they were thinking about escaping. But where? Switzerland?" Marcel knew that Switzerland was a neutral country and not involved in the war.

"Not Switzerland," Papa said. "The border is too far from here, and it's too dangerous for them to head north; the Nazis have taken over Paris. And they can't go anywhere in the Mediterranean by boat, either. Too many guards looking for Jewish refugees."

"So then what would they do?" asked Marcel.

"Cross the Pyrenees, and into Spain," he said. "Though that has its own risks. The mountain terrain is very rugged. And it's December—there'll be snow on the ground. Border police will be patrolling all the time. Soldiers, too. They have dogs. But I know it's possible because it's been done. Our people have been able to arrange it."

"How long would that take?" asked Marcel.

"It depends on the weather," said Papa. "It could be a night's journey. Maybe two."

"You have access to this girl," Maman said. "Go to her house—right now. Don't let anyone see you. Tell the family that they have to be ready to leave at a moment's notice. They can't take much with them, though. And they can't let it be known that they are fleeing."

Papa nodded, and added, "We'll have to speak to some people and make some inquiries. We'll put a plan into action, but we need a few hours. You had better hurry."

Marcel looked at the grave, worried faces of his parents. They were clearly worn-out, but determined, too. He didn't exactly want to go. The image of the Gestapo officers was fresh in his mind and he was scared. But how could he let them down? Or Delphine? "I'll ride my bike over there," Marcel said. "I can leave right now."

In a furious rush, Marcel pedaled down the cold, dark streets. He wore all black, the better to blend in with the night. He saw no one, and he prayed that no one had spotted him and wondered where he was going and why. It wasn't just gendarmes or soldiers he had to worry about. Like Thierry's parents, plenty of people in town supported the new regime headed by Pétain. Informers were everywhere.

He'd never actually been to Delphine's house before but she had told him where it was and what it looked like, so he was able to find it without much trouble. It was a small, slightly run-down structure, and when he saw it, he remembered it had belonged to an old man who had lived there for a very long time. After the man died a couple of years ago, no one else moved in. People said the man had a son in Lille but that he never came here. The house had sat empty until Delphine's family moved there.

Marcel stashed his bicycle by the gate and approached the house swiftly. He saw a light in what seemed to be the kitchen, and through the window, he could see a dark-haired woman moving around. That had to be Delphine's mother. He'd never met her or any of the other members of her family before. Well, it was time to meet them now. He knocked softly on the door.

"Who is it?" A voice called. It sounded suspicious.

"Marcel. I'm a friend of Delphine's."

"Wait here," said the voice. A couple of moments later, the door opened. There stood Delphine, with the dark-haired woman right behind her.

"It's all right, Maman," said Delphine. "Marcel's my friend. He won't hurt us." She let Marcel inside.

"How do you know?" blazed her mother. "He could be an informer; the town is crawling with spies—"

"I'm not an informer," said Marcel. "My parents— they're in the Resistance. They sent me to help you." He straightened up, trying to stand as tall he could.

"You see?" Delphine said. "I told you!"

"I'm sorry," said Delphine's mother. "I'm just so on edge. After what happened at school today, I've been in a panic."

"That stupid photograph!" cried Delphine. "I didn't even know it was in the bag. I put it there so long ago that I'd forgotten all about it. And now it's my fault we've been exposed. Everything is all my fault!" She began to cry.

"Don't say that, *ma chère*," said her mother, putting an arm around her. "You couldn't have known. None of us could. We can't think about what's already happened.

We have to think about the future. Your friend Marcel—he was brave to come here. Now you have to be brave, too."

Delphine sniffed and wiped her eyes. "You're right," she said to her mother. And then to Marcel, "Do you have a message for us? Is there a plan?"

"My parents are working on it right now. They said to tell you to be ready to leave at any time, but not to make it look like you are fleeing. I'll be back as soon as I have something to tell you."

Delphine listened attentively, nodding as he spoke. Then she asked, "Why is your family doing all this?"

"Because we have to," he said. "It's the right thing to do. We can't just give in to . . . *them*. We can't."

"We're grateful they feel that way," said a deep voice. Marcel turned to see a man with a short, dark beard enter the room. Delphine's father. "Not everyone does. There are plenty of French people who are supporting the Germans. They're only too happy to turn us in. We've got to get out of here."

"My father said something about going over the mountains, into Spain," said Marcel.

"But it's so dangerous!" said Delphine's mother.

Marcel said nothing. She was right. He had studied those mountains, the Pyrenees, in geography. Like Papa had said, the terrain was steep and rocky. There would be snow, ice, and freezing winds. Wild animals lived in the forest. And, of course, there would be soldiers combing the paths. They might have fierce, sharp-nosed dogs along with them.

Marcel wished he could say something that would sound encouraging. But all he could think of was "I'll be back. You can count on me."

TEN

The next morning, Marcel woke with the light. Last night before bed, Papa had told him about the message he needed to bring to the Resistance member in the neighboring town.

Still rubbing his eyes, he went into the kitchen. He could smell the bread his mother had baked: a round peasant loaf and the *pain d'épice* the soldier liked so much. He knew it was hard getting supplies to bake anything these days, and shelves of the bakery were often empty or nearly so.

Marcel ate breakfast while she wrapped up the baked goods. She put the loaf in a white cloth and the *pain d'épice* in a checked cloth. "Remember, if they ask, give the soldiers the *pain d'épice*," she said. "Maybe they won't even bother with you today."

It was the day honoring Saint François-Xavier. He was born in Navarre, in Spain, but was well-known and loved in the entire region. The holiday was widely celebrated and school would be closed. Everyone would be in church and not focused on Marcel or where he happened to be going on his bike.

"Don't worry," he told his mother. "I'll remember." Both she and his father stepped outside to watch him as he pedaled off down the road.

It had rained the night before and there was still a fine mist hovering over everything as Marcel rode down the cobblestone street, heading out of town. There was a slight nip in the air, too. He wished he'd remembered to wear gloves. But he just pedaled harder, relying on his own body to create warmth and power. That was what the riders in the Tour de France would have done. Every victory they achieved came from their own personal sense of determination.

Once Marcel had reached the outskirts of town, he turned left, away from the direction of the bridge. This was a different route, not one he usually took. But this was the direction his father had outlined in his instructions. The road here was very bumpy. It was also slippery from the rain, and from all the wet leaves that were plastered everywhere.

As he rounded a curve, the bike went over an especially big bump and the loaf of bread flew out of the basket, flipped over, and landed right smack in the center of a shallow puddle. *Zut!* Marcel jumped off the bicycle and hurried over to inspect the damage. The muddy water had seeped through the white cloth and into the bread. He peeled away the cloth and blotted the loaf against his pants. Then he remounted and continued on his way. As he rode, he looked down at the contents of his basket. The bread still looked all right. Thank goodness. Besides, he had the *pain d'épice* if he needed something to offer.

Soon he found himself on the main road into town. The central square was filled with people coming from church. Many of them were on bicycles as well.

But the square was filled with something else, too, something terrifying. Rolling right up the main street was an armored truck! The soldiers driving it were clearly German. What were they doing here? Looking for Jews to . . . deport?

Marcel wanted to get out of there as quickly as he could, but a French gendarme stationed under an equestrian statue of General Napoleon caught sight of him and gestured for him to come over.

Marcel was nervous as he obeyed the gendarme's command. "What do you have there?" the gendarme asked.

"Bread, sir." He hoped he didn't sound too scared.

"And where are you taking it?"

Marcel was silent. He did not want to say where he was going. He might put the Resistance member in danger if he did. But before he could answer, another gendarme came by and they began arguing—it seemed to be about whose turn it was to do something. The question about where Marcel was going was apparently forgotten—at least for now. Marcel was just about to ask if he could leave when one of the gendarmes looked into his basket.

"Smells good," he commented. "I want a piece."

Marcel's mouth went bone-dry with terror. The gendarme was pointing at the loaf of bread that contained the note!

"No, you idiot, forget the bread. We can get bread anywhere. Look what else he's got—I can smell it." The second gendarme was opening the checked cloth to reveal the *pain d'épice.*

"Take it," Marcel urged, praying they would forget about the other loaf. "My mother made it and it's really good. Everyone says so. She's known for her *pain d'épice.* Famous, even. " He was babbling now, his nervousness causing him to talk, talk, talk.

"Merci," said the gendarme as he tucked the bundle under his arm. "Maybe we should take both?" he asked his comrade.

Marcel went stiff as a plank with panic. These men were cooperating with the Germans. If the gendarme took the loaf, he'd find the note! Then what? His imagination painted horrible pictures: his parents dragged from their home, interrogated, maybe even tortured. Or killed.

"Nah, let's leave something for the kid, right?" He leaned over to give Marcel a gentle punch on the arm. "Go on home now. And say thanks to your famous mom."

Dumbly, Marcel nodded. As he sped off, the wheels of the bike seemed to be chanting this refrain: *almost caught, almost caught, almost caught*. But he *didn't* get caught, he reminded himself. He was still free, still all right, and the note was still in the loaf of bread. Now it was up to him to deliver it.

After he'd been told to go home, Marcel didn't want the gendarmes to see him still pedaling around, so he rode back the way he'd come in, and then circled all around the edges of town for almost an hour, trying to find another way to get in. Now he was behind schedule, but there was nothing he could do. Finally, he discovered a small hidden path near a cemetery. The moss-covered headstones dotting the grass looked ancient. Many were crumbling, cracked, or tilted. He slowed to read a few of the dates: 1851, 1807, 1899. If he'd had more time, he would have gone in to explore. It was spooky in there, and looked interesting. But he didn't dare stop. Not now.

After following the narrow path into the town, he kept riding around until he found the right street. And there, on the corner, was the clock and watch repair shop his father had described to him. A big pocket watch was painted on the sign out front, just as he'd said. The shop was closed but Marcel used special code: three fast knocks, a pause, and two slow knocks. His father said this was necessary because the person in the shop did not know him personally.

There was a long silence during which he had to wonder if he was in the right place after all. Then finally someone came to the door and opened it a crack. When the man behind the door saw Marcel standing there, he opened it wider and, without a word, gestured for Marcel to come inside and to bring his bicycle.

The man was tall and slightly stooped, with silver hair and silver-rimmed glasses. Marcel's father had described him perfectly. What he had not mentioned was that the man's ankle was heavily bandaged, and he was using a cane. Marcel offered the man the remaining loaf of bread. *"Bonjour, monsieur,"* he said, just as his father had instructed. "I have a small gift for you. It's very tasty French bread and I think you will enjoy it very much."

The man took the bread. He understood the message, and its emphasis on the word *French*. He, like Marcel's parents, was opposed to the German Occupation. *"Merci beaucoup,"* he said. "Will you excuse me for a minute?" He disappeared through a door behind the counter, leaving Marcel to wait in the shop. Marcel knew he would read the message and then destroy it.

While waiting, Marcel looked around the shop. There were clocks and watches of every description: clocks that sat on mantels, clocks that hung on walls. There was a cuckoo clock and a grandfather clock. And the glass cases were filled with watches. He leaned over to see them better. He'd love to have a stopwatch, so he could time himself on the bike. Maybe one day . . .

The man returned. He was frowning. "We have a problem," he said. "There was an accident on the mountain road last night. A big truck carrying crates of chickens overturned. Another driver was speeding and didn't see the downed truck in the dark. He hit it, and the truck went up in flames. The fire spread before the fire truck got there, and it took them several hours to put it out. Now the whole area is a mess: The road is water-logged, and there are branches all over the place. There's even a downed tree. And let's not forget the chickens that they're still trying to round up. It won't be safe for the family to go until everything's back to normal."

"But they have to get out of town immediately. They can't stay where they are—someone at school exposed the girl."

"Hmm," said the man. "If that's true, then someone at the school will have already contacted the gendarmes."

"Maybe not. It is a holiday," Marcel pointed out.

"You could be right." The man looked hard at Marcel, as if sizing him up. "This family—you say they need a place to stay. Maybe I can arrange that. *Maybe.* But I'd have to get a message to another one of our people. Ordinarily, I'd go myself but I can't," he said, and gestured toward his wounded ankle. "Can you do it instead?"

Marcel hesitated. He was already running late. His parents, especially his mother, would be worried about him being gone so long. But who could have predicted that the truck would have overturned? Or that the silver-haired man wouldn't be able to deliver a message himself? "I'll do it," he said. "Just tell me where to go."

"All right," said the man. "But I don't want to give you a note. It's too dangerous. You'll have to memorize what I'm going to tell you. And then you'll have to memorize whatever information the contact gives you."

"I memorized the information that got me here," said Marcel. "I can memorize this, too."

"Head to Port-Vendres. When you get to the center of town, face the big church with the stained glass window. Take a right turn at that corner. Go three more streets, and then take a left. Continue on that street until you come to a stone house with black shutters and white lace curtains."

Marcel nodded. "I'll remember," he said. "But that takes me farther from home, so I'll get back much later than I thought. My parents will be worried."

"I'd offer to telephone your parents, but you know that's not safe."

Marcel knew why—the few telephones in town were party lines, which meant that they were hardly private.

Resistance members would not dare to communicate that way.

Since there was no way to reach his parents, Marcel got back on his bicycle, heading toward the coastal town of Port-Vendres, about ten kilometers away. He rode swiftly, intent on reaching his destination as soon as he could. He'd have a long way back, and the days were so short now. He'd probably have to ride home in the dark.

He'd never been this far from home before, and he tried to keep an eye out for landmarks, just in case he needed them on the return trip. There was a stone church with a bell tower. There was a pasture with a low fence. Behind it, a white horse grazed peacefully. He'd just come to the center of a small village when the bike must have gone over something sharp, because suddenly he was wobbling this way and that, the bike weaving out of control. He stopped and jumped off to inspect. No! His back tire was flat! It couldn't be. It just couldn't. No, no, *no*!

Marcel looked wildly around. It was a holiday. Even if the town had a bike shop, which he highly doubted, it would be closed. What was he going to do? His fear quickly mounted to full-blown panic. He had to get the message through. He had to.

He began to walk the bike through the town square. It was pretty quiet now. Church services were over and everyone was back at home having lunch or a nap. Then he spied a boy pedaling toward him. The boy looked like he was around ten or eleven, and he rode a black, very battered-looking bike.

The boy stopped when he was face-to-face with Marcel. "What's wrong?" he asked. "Did you get a flat?"

"Yeah," said Marcel. "I did. I don't suppose you have a spare tire I could use?"

The boy shook his head. "Sorry. Anything we had we gave to the soldiers. If we didn't they would have taken it anyway." He made a disgusted face.

"I know what you mean," Marcel said, an idea beginning to form in his mind. "What about switching bikes with me?" he asked.

"Switch bikes with you? Why would I want to do that?"

"Because I'm going to my aunt's house in Port-Vendres," said Marcel, inventing a story on the spot. "I have a really important message for her. It's urgent, in fact. My cousin is really sick."

"I don't know . . . ," said the boy.

Marcel could tell he was wavering. "I have to get this message to her. My cousin—she might even die."

That got the boy's attention. Clearly, he believed Marcel's story, so Marcel was encouraged to go on. "Please help me out," he wheedled. And then he added, "Look, my bike is in much better shape than yours. No dents, and hardly any scratches or nicks. And it has a basket."

"A basket would be handy," said the boy.

"Sure it would!" He patted the basket. "Look how big it is."

"I could put a lot of stuff in there . . ." The boy seemed to be thinking out loud.

"You'd be getting a really good deal," coaxed Marcel. "A great deal, in fact."

"All right," said the boy firmly. "I'll do it."

"Thank you!" cried Marcel. He had to stop himself from pushing the boy away from the bike—that was how eager he was to get going again.

"Good luck," said the boy. "I hope everything works out with your cousin. Do you really think she's going to die?"

But Marcel was already on his way. He couldn't afford to slow down his trip for even the few seconds it would take to turn around and answer the question. Or wave farewell.

Marcel was already worn-out from the morning's events, and the ride to Port-Vendres was punishing. He was exhausted, and very, very cold. But then he thought of the riders in the Tour de France. Surely they got tired, hungry, and cold, too. They had to ride in all kinds of weather—extreme heat and freezing cold. Rain, snow, and hail.

And surely they must have lost faith sometimes, doubting their own ability to win or even finish. But did they give up? No, they did not. They kept on pedaling. Marcel admired those riders more than he admired anyone in the whole world. And for that reason, he made them both his model and his inspiration. They did not give up, and neither would he. This was his own Tour de France, one of the most difficult stages. No matter how bad it got, he would not stop riding. He would keep on going until he reached the finish line—his destination—and delivered his message.

It was mid-afternoon by the time he reached Port-Vendres. The wind in this coastal town was even sharper. The town was also bigger than he expected, and even with the instructions of the silver-haired man, it took him a while to find the stone house with the black shutters and the white lace curtains.

When he used the special knock on the door, it was answered by a short, plump woman with brown curls escaping from her bun. Her skin was very brown, too, and there were tiny wrinkles at the corners of her eyes. "I'm here about the clock," he began, wanting to be sure he said exactly the right thing. "It's not working and won't be fixed for at least another day."

"I wasn't expecting you." She looked at him suspiciously. "Are you sure you're in the right place?"

"I'm here to make sure the clock gets fixed as soon as possible. There are people depending on it." This is what the man in the clock repair shop had instructed him to say.

"I see," she said, looking him over. "And the clock, where is it from?"

"Oh, it's a French clock, madame," he said.

The woman looked at him steadily. "Then it must be a good clock. When it's ready, can you bring it to another house in town? I'll let you know exactly where."

"Sure," said Marcel. "Is it far from here?"

"No," said the woman. "It's in Saint-Girons, the next town over. My husband will be there to receive the delivery. The clock can stay there until it's time to bring it home."

Marcel breathed a small sigh of relief. He'd gotten the message right. The woman had understood his coded words and given him a coded message of her own in reply. Her husband would greet Delphine's family when they got to the house, where they would spend the night. Then they would continue on their way to Spain through the mountain pass as soon as the chickens had been captured and the truck was gone.

"What's the name of the street?" he asked.

"Rue des Bois," she said.

"Rue des Bois," repeated Marcel, committing the name to memory. Then he asked, "What does the house look like?"

"It's stone, like this one. And the door is painted dark red. There's a barn out back, and to the left of the house, a vegetable garden. Can you remember all that?"

"Dark red door. Barn. Vegetable garden. I'll remember. Tell your husband thank you. The clock is very valuable. It's important to handle it carefully."

"He will," said the woman. "He's never broken a clock yet. Or lost one."

"I'm really glad to hear that," Marcel said. He was about to get going again when she put a hand on his arm. "You look cold. Can I give you a sweater for the ride home? And some gloves?"

"A sweater and gloves would be great," he said. He waited by the door while she went inside. A few minutes later she returned with a nubby, hand-knit sweater, hand-knit gloves, and a slice of a baguette and a thick wedge of cheese wrapped in a cloth.

"Thank you for all the information about the clock delivery," she said. "I appreciate it." Then she added, "Have a safe trip home."

"*Merci*," he said as he slipped on the sweater and the gloves. He no longer had a basket, so he tied the bundle of food tightly to the handlebars. His stomach rumbled loudly. But his fear—of being stopped by soldiers, of failing Delphine and her family—was even greater than his hunger. He had to get on the road again to deliver his new information as soon as possible.

ELEVEN

Marcel rode back toward Aucoin like a demon, as fast and hard as he could. His legs burned with the exertion. But he knew from all his reading that the way a cyclist handled that burn was the key to his becoming a better rider. Marcel was determined to work through it, like a real Tour de France cyclist. He wouldn't let it stop him.

Dark came quickly, along with a cold and stinging rain. The bike he had traded for was not as good as his old bike, so he had trouble maneuvering over some of the rougher patches. Still, Tour de France riders didn't stop for rain, and neither did he. He kept going, not even stopping to eat the cheese and bread he'd been given.

It was a good thing he'd thought to watch out for landmarks on the way there, because without the sunlight, things were harder to remember. But look, there was the pasture, though the horse was no longer outside, grazing. He must be safe in his stall for the night. Lucky horse! Then he saw the church he had passed on his way. That meant he was headed in the right direction. He decided to stop in the church for a few minutes—just long enough to eat the bread and cheese. But when he pushed open the church door, wheeled in the bike, and sat down in an empty pew, he realized the little package was not there—it must have fallen off along the way.

Discouraged, Marcel left the church. The rain had stopped, but he was still wet and cold. Well, the Tour de France riders probably got wet and cold, too. He got back on his bike and began to ride again, pushing himself hard, and then harder still. In his head, he could see the crowd and hear their cheers as he passed. The fatigue he felt was the fatigue of the long-distance rider, and like that rider, he would keep on going.

After what seemed like hours, Marcel found himself on the road that led back to Aucoin. It had a slight incline, but he was so tired that it felt like a mountain. But he pushed on. *Almost there, almost there . . .*

Then, just as he was about to turn onto the familiar cobblestone street that led to the bakery and his home, the bike hit something—and it was something big! The dark made it impossible to see what it was. All he knew was that he was pitched forward off the bike, and head-first onto the hard, unforgiving ground. Ow! His glasses came off when he fell, and he had to crawl and feel around for a few frantic moments until he found them and put them back on. The frames were a bit bent, but at least he could see again. What a relief.

Slowly, Marcel pulled himself up. His knees were skinned and his hands were bloody. And he hurt all over, including his head, which he'd also hit when he fell. His legs felt too weak to ride, so he started walking his bike instead.

As he approached the bakery, he looked up to the window above the shop. The lights were on—there were his parents, huddled together. They must have been looking out for him, anxiously awaiting his return. He'd never been so glad to see them in his life. He was still shaken from the accident, but quietly triumphant, too. Like one of his cyclist heroes, he had made it to the finish.

When his parents spotted him, they turned and rushed from the window. They were downstairs and in the street in a matter of seconds.

"What happened?" cried his father. "You were gone so long!" Then he looked at the wreck of a bicycle Marcel had wheeled home. After the fall, the traded bicycle was in even worse shape than it had been when he'd gotten it. "And what's this? Where is your bicycle?" his father asked.

"Never mind about the bicycle now!" said his mother. "Can't you see he's been hurt?" She threw her arms around him. He welcomed the hug, but oh, how he ached.

They helped him up the stairs to their apartment, where it was safe and warm. But he was still shivering, and though he took off the gloves, he kept the sweater on. "Can I have something to eat?" Marcel asked. He thought of his bread and cheese, lying somewhere on the road from Port-Vendres. "Something hot? I'll tell you everything, but I'm so hungry!"

"Of course!" His mother hurried to prepare him a plate of food, while his father brought warm water and soap to clean his wounds and gauze to bandage them. Then his mother put down the plate in front of him. But as hungry as he'd been, he was able to eat only a few mouthfuls. He was feeling too dazed and sick to manage any more than that.

"It's all right," said Maman, removing the food. "Maybe just some hot milk. I'll heat it up now."

"Can you tell us what happened?" asked Papa.

"I'll try," said Marcel. For suddenly it seemed like this day was so much longer than the actual hours that made it up, and that the distance he'd traveled was so very, very far. He felt like he'd been gone for days. Or even a week.

"It was really slippery and wet on the road," he began. "The loaf of bread bounced out of the basket and into a mud puddle. But luckily it only got a little soggy. And then I got stopped by some soldiers, and they almost took it."

"But they didn't?" Papa's face was pinched with fear.

Marcel nodded. "In the end, they let me keep it and only took the *pain d'épice*."

"It's worked every time. I knew it would work again." Maman came to the table with a small bowl of steamed milk. She'd added just a little bit of sugar from their increasingly precious supply. "No one can resist my *pain d'épice*."

Marcel sipped the milk. It felt good going down. "They told me to go home. I didn't want them to see me again so I took the long way around the town. Then I found the clock shop and the man you told me about. I gave him the bread and he took it away to read the note. But when he came back he said there had been an accident on the mountain road."

"What kind of accident?" asked Maman. She was sitting next to him at the table. Papa was on his other side. They were drinking in every word.

"A truck hit another truck and started a fire. There's water all over the place, along with dead branches and a downed tree. And there was something about some escaped chickens, too."

"It will take a little time to clear all that up," said Maman.

"Yes. And so the road was going to be very busy. The man said Delphine and her family would need to wait before trying to cross the border. But he'd hurt his ankle, so he couldn't ride to give the message to the people with the safe house. He asked me to do it."

"You!" exclaimed Papa. "Where did you have to go?"

"Port-Vendres," said Marcel.

"That's so far," his father said. "But you did it. You did it!"

"Yes!" Marcel smiled. "I went to see a woman the clockmaker told me about. He gave me a message for her, and she told me about the house where Delphine's family could spend the night."

"And where is that?" Papa asked eagerly. "We want to let them know the plan as soon as possible."

"It's in Saint-Girons."

"Saint-Girons makes sense," said his father. "It's not too far from the border. What about the house?"

Marcel thought hard, trying to remember all the details. "The house—it's made of stone. And the door is . . ." But what was the color of the door? Black? Dark blue? Green? He suddenly couldn't recall.

"Can you think of it?" his father asked gently.

"I'm not sure," he said. There had been so many things to remember today: houses, people, highly important messages. There had been a church, and a pasture with a white horse. Or did he imagine that?

"It will come to you," Maman said. "Do you remember anything else? The name of the street?"

"The name of the street is . . ." Marcel was stumped. He knew this, he *did*. He even remembered repeating it, to be sure he would not forget. And yet, the actual name of the street stubbornly refused to take shape in his mind. "I don't know," he said miserably. "I just can't think of what it is!"

He caught a glimpse of the look that passed back and forth between his parents. This was bad. Very bad. He knew it and they knew it, too. But they tried, for his sake, to be encouraging and not show how worried they were.

"Get some rest," his mother said. "If you sleep for a little while, your mind will be clearer."

"What if it's not?" he said. "Delphine and her family will be captured and deported if I can't remember!"

"Don't think that way." His mother tried to lead him from the table to his room. But he refused to let her.

"I can't sleep now," he said. "Not until I remember the name of the street and what the house looks like. There is something out front and maybe something out back too . . ."

"Nothing can happen tonight anyway," said his father. "It's so late it will be morning soon. Your mother is right. Go to sleep. Things will be better when you get up. You'll see." He nudged Marcel out of his seat and toward his room, and this time Marcel allowed himself to be led. But the worry was as strong as the fatigue. "What if I don't remember?" Marcel said. "Then what?"

His parents had no good answer for this. *Of course not*, he thought grimly. *There is none.* He trudged into his room, where he undressed and let his clothes drop straight to the floor in a heap. He was so tired he didn't even care that his mother would scold him for leaving them there. Then he climbed into bed. He did not expect to sleep—he did not even *want* to sleep. But sleep overtook him anyway, and even in his dreams, his mind was busy trying to piece together the elements of the day.

He dreamed of a truck overturned in the road, its wheels spinning and spinning. The wheels turned into clocks. The clocks turned into chickens with flapping wings ... then there was a horse, a cow, and a pig. A hunk of cheese, a loaf of bread ... He bolted up in bed, at once cold and hot. His teeth chattered but his face felt like it was on fire. Why couldn't he remember? Why?

Marcel got up, went to the window, and opened the shutters. The night sky was clear and soft, like black velvet. The stars twinkled, bright but distant. Just looking at them calmed him a bit. Then he saw the pitcher of water and the glass his mother had put on his desk. He filled it to the brim and guzzled it down. There. That was better. Then he returned to bed. He *would* remember the house, the street—everything—when he awoke. Or else if he didn't, he'd go riding back the entire way to get the message again.

TWELVE

It was not quite dawn when Marcel opened his eyes. He could see the sky's slow brightening through the window, whose shutters he had not closed last night. He was calmer now. Without telling his parents, he had formed a new plan. He would ride back to Port-Vendres, right now, to the house of the woman who'd given him the message. And he would remember it this time, writing it all down if he had to. Not on a piece of paper, though. That was too dangerous. No, he would bring a pen and write on his skin if he needed to, somewhere under his clothes where no one would ever think to look.

It was true that the bicycle was not in great shape, but he had thought of that, too. He would ride over to Arnaud's house first. He knew his friend kept his bicycle unlocked in a small shed behind the house. He would borrow his friend's bike and return it later. Arnaud lived so close to school that he did not ride there, and he would never even know the bicycle was missing.

As Marcel stood there looking out the window, the sky grew brighter. The rain was over and it looked like it was turning into a nice day. Perfect for an early-morning ride. He had just reached for his pants and the still-damp jacket he'd worn home last night when his attention was snagged by the clip-clop of a horse's hooves outside in the street. There was the milkman in his wagon, delivering the glass bottles of milk along with the small containers of cream and butter all over town. Of course, there was no cream and not much milk these days. And no butter, either. Yet the milk-man continued to make his rounds, delivering whatever he could.

Marcel recognized the horse, an old brown mare with a weakness for peppermints and a long, thick tail she swished in rhythm as she walked. And the dark red wagon was familiar, too, its deep color coming to life as the sky grew lighter. Suddenly, it hit him like a bolt. The milk wagon was the *exact* color of the door in Saint-Girons! The door of the safe house where Delphine and her family were going to spend the night! And as soon as he remembered that, he remembered the name of the street, too: rue des Bois!

Marcel left the damp jacket where it was and pulled on the rest of his rumpled clothes, including the nubby sweater the woman had given him. Then he went to wake his father. Together, they put Marcel's bicycle into the bakery cart and drove to Delphine's house. They took the back streets, avoiding the center of town, and when they arrived, Papa waited some distance away while Marcel knocked on the door. "It's me, Marcel," he said in a low voice. It was only when Delphine's mother had opened the door that Marcel motioned for Papa to join them.

"Who is this?" said Delphine's mother, clearly alarmed.

"It's my father," Marcel said.

Papa extended his hand and Delphine's mother grasped it tightly in both of hers. "Thank you for helping us," she said. "It feels like a miracle." Delphine's father shook his hand as well.

Papa nodded to both of them. "Not all of us have fallen in league with the devil," he replied. Then he continued. "Can you leave right now? There's no time to waste."

Delphine's mother nodded eagerly.

"We knew this was coming, so we've eaten, and we have everything prepared," said Delphine's father.

"Warm boots? Warm clothes? Gloves, hats, and scarves?" Marcel's father asked. "It will be cold in the mountains."

"We have all that. Also a flashlight, batteries, a compass, and some rope—you never know when it might come in handy."

"I have dried fruit and some nuts," added Delphine's mother. "And we each have a canteen." She began moving around the room, gathering things as the men continued talking.

"That's good," said Marcel's father. "Now, what about money?"

"I have some," Delphine's father said. "And we have some jewelry, too." He turned to his wife. "Is everything sewn into the coats? The rings, your mother's pins and her earrings?"

"All done," she said.

"Then we can go," said Marcel's father. "I can't say who will be helping you along the way—the less any one of us in the chain knows, the better. But I do know there will be help. You may be offered a barn, a wine cellar, or even a cave. It will take us a few hours to get to the safe house. Then you'll have to go over the mountains to cross the border. It will take a day or two, and it won't be easy."

"We know," said Delphine's mother. "But we have no choice."

They all went outside, and as the men were loading backpacks into the bakery wagon, Marcel took Delphine aside.

"I won't see you again." He was surprised at how bad this made him feel. "Anyway, I hope you have a safe trip," he added.

"Thank you," she said.

There was a pause and then he asked, "Are you afraid?"

"So afraid!" she burst out.

"I understand," Marcel said. "I'd be afraid, too. But my father says these people have gotten other families out. They'll get yours out, too. Then you'll be in Spain."

"I don't speak Spanish," she said. "Not a single word."

"You're smart," he said. "You'll learn."

She gave him a tiny smile. "I hope so." Then she said, "Keep riding, okay?"

"I will." He looked around the yard. "Where's the bike?" He thought longingly of the shiny red bicycle and the gleaming silver bell.

"My father painted it black and then he sold it. He didn't want anyone to recognize it, in case they remembered seeing me on it."

"That was a good idea." But it made him sad. They would probably never race together again. Then he had another thought. "What about your cat?" Marcel remembered the orange cat he'd nearly hit, which was the first time he'd seen Delphine.

"My father is going to set her free," Delphine said. "He says she's a good hunter and she'll be all right." But since she looked like she was about to cry, she obviously didn't believe it.

"We'll take her," Marcel said impulsively. "We always need cats in the bakery. They keep the mice away."

"Oh, would you?" she said, clasping her hands together under her chin. "Could you?"

"I'll ask my father but I am sure he'll say yes," he said. And just then, he heard his father's voice, "Marcel, you'd better be getting on to school. Delphine and her family have to go now."

Marcel sighed. *"Adieu,"* he said. Unlike *au revoir,* which they said all the time, *adieu* was the word people used when they were saying good-bye forever. It sounded so mournful.

"Adieu," she echoed before walking over to the bakery wagon.

Marcel watched as the family climbed inside. His father piled the bags of flour and other supplies around them, concealing them as best he could. Then Marcel helped him lay a large piece of oilcloth over everything. Papa climbed onto the wagon and gave the signal to the horse. They were off on their journey. He could only hope and pray they reached their destination safely.

Marcel slowly walked over to retrieve his bicycle. He was surprised to feel the prick of tears. He pulled his glasses off and swiped at his eyes. Then he took a deep breath and looked around briefly for the cat. She was nowhere to be found—he would have to come back for her.

Marcel rode over toward the school on the wobbly bike, which he planned to hide in the alley by the flower shop. But there was Guillaume, swaggering up the street just as Marcel was dismounting.

"Hey, where did you get this old hunk of junk?" Guillaume gave the handlebars a little shake.

"None of your business," said Marcel darkly. Why did he have to be walking by at just this exact minute? What a rotten piece of luck.

"Well, wherever you got it, you should take it right back. It's a wreck."

"Like I don't know that," Marcel muttered.

"What happened to your bike?" Guillaume persisted.

"It . . . got crushed by a van." Marcel had to think fast.

"Seriously? Were you on it?"

"What are you, a dope or something? If I'd been on it, would I be here talking to you now? No, I'd left it parked and some stupid van backed right into it. The driver said he didn't even see it. It was squashed flat."

"Too bad," Guillaume said.

"Yeah, it was," agreed Marcel. Then, eager to change the subject, he added, "Did you hear? The school week is going to be cut to four days. To save on electricity and heat and stuff."

"Tu blagues!" You're kidding. Guillaume's eyes opened wide in surprise.

"Not that it's been decided or anything. Right now, it's just a rumor." *Yeah, a rumor I just started*, thought Marcel. And it worked. Guillaume had completely lost any interest in the subject of Marcel's old bike or his new one.

Marcel was proud of how he'd come up with that idea. But when he walked into the classroom and saw Delphine's empty seat, his warm glow of pride vanished in an instant.

THIRTEEN

At school that morning, Marcel just could *not* focus. He was exhausted from all the cycling yesterday, kilometer after kilometer, and from the fall he'd taken. And the room was freezing. Coal had been strictly rationed and now the classroom was never warm enough. Some days it was so chilly that Mademoiselle Babineaux let them keep their coats on. Maybe the school *would* be shut down one day a week, and his little lie to Guillaume would turn out not to be a lie after all.

He thought of Delphine and her family in the bakery wagon. They were on just the first leg of a long and dangerous journey. Would they be able to get through to Port-Vendres or would they be discovered? And if they were, what would happen to Delphine and her family? And to Papa? Jews were not the only ones in danger. The people who helped them were, too.

"Wake up, Marcel," Mademoiselle Babineaux said when he'd been drifting off. "You need to give us your attention."

The class tittered and Marcel felt his face go pink. This was going to be a long, long day. The clock hanging at the front of the classroom said nine thirty. That meant even lunch was more than two hours away. Would the time ever go by? The hands on the clock seemed to be glued in place. Maybe it was broken.

Then two Gestapo officers walked into the classroom. Suddenly, Marcel was awake and alert. Did their appearance have anything to do with Delphine's absence? He dared not look over at Delphine's empty seat, but it was an effort not to.

The officers walked up to Mademoiselle Babineaux's desk. One of them leaned over and quietly said something. She stood up. "Class, I am going into the corridor for a few minutes. Paulette, you're in charge. Everyone will study the spelling words while I'm gone."

Marcel was so nervous that he couldn't grasp the words in his notebook. They looked like nonsense, and had no meaning. What were they saying out there? Was it about Delphine?

Mademoiselle Babineaux came back into the room. The officers were not with her, and Marcel felt his stomach unclench—until he heard her next words.

"Delphine is not here today," she remarked. "Does anyone know where she is?"

Marcel didn't know what to do. He did not want to reveal that he was friends with Delphine and because of this, might know where she was. On the other hand, he wanted to help her by saying something that would quell any suspicions his teacher might have about her. What was the right thing to say? What should he do?

He raised his hand.

"Yes, Marcel? You know something?"

Why did that question sound so threatening? "Yes, mademoiselle," he said. "Remember she was sick the other day and had to go home early? She's still sick. That's why she's not here."

"And how do you know that?" she asked.

Marcel panicked. He had not thought of that and had to scramble to come up with an answer. "Her mother came into the bakery and told my mother," he said finally.

"That's not true!" Thierry called out. "She's a dirty Jew and he's friends with her. Maybe he's even hiding her at his house!"

"Thierry!" said Mademoiselle Babineaux. "You're not to call out without raising your hand. Be quiet until I've given you permission to speak." Then she turned to Marcel. "Come with me into the hall for a moment?" She looked at Paulette. "I'm counting on you to keep order here."

Marcel felt his mouth go dry and his hands go clammy. He was going to have to talk to the Gestapo officers! Answer their questions! If he said or did *anything* suspicious, he could put Delphine, her family, and his own parents in grave danger.

The two officers stood waiting in the corridor. They wore dark, belted uniforms with breeches that were tucked into their boots. One was very blond, and he spoke first. "Do you know this girl Delphine Gilette?"

"Yes, sir." Marcel was so frightened the words came out as no more than a whisper.

"Speak up," said the officer curtly. "I can't hear you."

"Yes, sir," Marcel repeated.

"Were you close friends with her? Did you know her family?"

"I knew her at school," he said. That was true at least.

"We've had a tip that she and her family are Jewish. Did you know this?" said the other officer sternly.

Marcel thought this might have been the hardest, most scary moment in his whole life, even scarier than when the soldiers almost took the loaf of bread with the note concealed. He had to be brave and strong, like his parents. Like his heroes in the Tour de France. He looked up at the officer. "No, sir," he said clearly. "I didn't."

The officer looked unsure whether to believe him or not. He turned to Mademoiselle Babineaux. "What's your sense here? Is he lying? Does he know something he's not telling us?"

There was a long, horrible silence in which Mademoiselle Babineaux said nothing. Marcel knew she liked him. He was a good student and never caused trouble like some of the other kids in class. But he also knew that she, like everyone, was frightened of the Gestapo. "Marcel is a good boy," she said finally. "If he says he didn't know about this family's true origins, I believe him."

The two officers looked at him. Marcel made himself look back. The blond officer looked away first. "All right, then. We've been to their house and we'll pursue other leads. If you do find out anything," he said to Marcel, "you'd better come forward right away. Is that clear?"

"Yes, sir," said Marcel.

"You may return to your desk," said Mademoiselle Babineaux.

Before he turned to go, he noticed her hands were shaking. He understood. He went inside and sat down at his desk, flooded with relief. His legs were jelly, his stomach a storm-tossed sea. But for the moment, he was safe.

The day stretched on. Every time there was a noise, Marcel's eyes went straight for the door. What if the Gestapo figured out he was lying and came back? What would happen then?

Finally, the bell rang, announcing lunch. Marcel sat at a table in the lunchroom, surrounded by his usual group of friends. He mostly listened to the conversation around him, smiling or laughing when it seemed right to do that and not adding very much of his own.

Then Thierry came up to the table. "I'll bet you knew from the beginning that she was a Jew, and you never said. You helped her hide. Or maybe even escape. And you know what *that* means." He made his hand into the shape of a pistol and pointed it to his head.

"Prove it," Marcel said.

"I don't have to," said Thierry. "They'll find her. They'll find her and then you'll see."

When he left, Guillaume asked softly, "What was the real reason she wasn't in school? Do you know?"

"It's like I said: She's still sick."

"You two are pretty good friends. I saw you riding with her a couple of times."

"So what if I did?" asked Marcel.

Guillaume gave him a pitying look. "Do I have to spell it out for you? She's a Jew. And everyone knows it's *not* a good idea to be friends with Jews. I mean, I feel sorry for her and all. And I didn't snitch, like Thierry. But you have to be careful, too, you know."

Marcel wanted to yell at him. Or even better yet, punch him. Hard. But what good would that do? He'd only get in trouble. And it might endanger Delphine and her family even more. So he abruptly stood up, pushing the table away as he did. Everything on the table shook and a glass of milk tipped over, pooling across the surface and dripping down into Guillaume's lap. Good.

"Hey, look what you did!" fumed Guillaume. "You better come back and help clean up this mess!"

But Marcel had already walked away. He did not look back. *Stay calm*, he told himself. *Just stay calm.*

After lunch, there was mathematics, history, and music. They still did not sing the French national anthem—that had stopped back in November—but they sang another traditional song and one after that. Finally, the seemingly endless day was over and he rushed home as soon as he could. He told his mother what had happened in school with the Gestapo officers.

"Mon Dieu!" she cried. "You must have been so frightened!"

"I was," he admitted.

"But you didn't tell."

"No, I didn't."

"You did a fine thing today," she said. "I'm proud of you. Very proud. And Papa will be, too." She gave Marcel a quick, tight hug.

"Now what?" he asked his mother.

"We wait for Papa to come back. That's all we can do."

Waiting, thought Marcel, may have been the hardest thing of all. He felt so powerless. It was a terrible feeling. But eventually, the afternoon faded to dusk.

"Do you think they're all right?" he asked his mother for the tenth time as he set the table with only two plates for supper. Who knew when—or if—his father would be back?

"I am praying that they are," she said. "I gave him bread, and a loaf of *pain d'épice*, too. I even baked some croissants this morning."

"Croissants? How did you do that?" Marcel asked.

Butter was in short supply and the croissant recipe required a lot of it.

"I've been hoarding butter in case I needed it for an emergency. So I mixed what I had with some margarine. Those German soldiers won't be able to tell the difference!"

"That should help," said Marcel. The baked goods would distract attention from the other things—and people—in the wagon. And even a regular loaf of fresh bread would help buy a little goodwill from a soldier.

Marcel and his mother sat down to eat. Food was in such short supply that they were always very hungry at mealtime. His mother had managed to get a tiny bit of rabbit and had made a stew with pieces of carrot in it. They ate every last bit of it.

Then Marcel helped his mother by wiping down the table without even being asked. After the meal, she turned on the radio and they sat listening to the news from Paris. None of it was good. The war was intensifying, and cities were being bombed. Maman switched off the radio. Marcel tried to concentrate on his homework but soon gave up. Even his cycling magazines held no appeal tonight. His mother sat sewing, though he noticed that a lot of the time her hands just sat in her lap, the needle glinting in the lamplight. They both kept looking at the clock on the mantel.

"When do you think he'll be back?" Marcel asked yet again.

"I'm not sure," said his mother. She put the sewing basket aside. "Maybe around ten o'clock." But the evening dragged on, and ten o'clock came and went with no sign of Papa. And soon it was almost eleven. It wasn't all that far to Port-Vendres and back. Surely his father should be home by now.

"Something could have happened," said Marcel.

"Anything could have happened," said his mother. "There's no way for us to know."

Then Marcel remembered the time not long ago when there had been a problem with the wagon wheel. Could there be an issue like that now? One that might even be delaying his trip? He told his mother his theory.

"You could be right," she said.

"Let me ride along the road to look for him. I can bring his tools. I'll put them in my satchel."

"No," said his mother. "It's not safe."

"But what about Papa?" Marcel pointed out. "Is *he* safe? And if he's not, isn't it up to us to help him?"

His mother did not have a good answer to this. She sat there silently. He could see she was thinking it over. "All right," she said finally. "You can go. But wait." She got up, went into the bedroom she shared with his father, and returned. "Take this with you." She handed him a small gold tin.

"What is it?"

"Touron," said his mother.

"Where did you get it?" he asked. *Touron* was a fancy marzipan roll that came in all kinds of colors and designs. Packed with pistachios, hazelnuts, and candied fruit, it was usually sold in slices and considered a very special treat. Marcel had only had it a few times in his life. There was nowhere in town to get it, though.

Especially now. So this must have come from some-where else.

"It was a gift. I was saving it. I thought it might come in handy."

Marcel took the tin. "All right, Maman," he said. "I'll take it with me."

She followed him down the stairs and outside. There was the bicycle, looking even worse for the wear. Marcel realized that before he set out, he'd need to adjust the handlebars and tighten the front wheel. He could not risk getting stuck somewhere on the road with all those tools in his bag. It might look very suspicious.

Marcel did not know a great deal about fixing bi-cycles, but Delphine had shown him how to check for a few of the most common problems and how to deal with them, too. She had known an awful lot about bicycles, and he tried to remember what she had told him. After about a half hour of tinkering, he had tightened the front wheel and realigned the handlebars so they weren't veering off course.

His mother stood watching as he adjusted his satchel and retied the scarf he was wearing around his neck. "Be safe," she said. "Go with God."

"I'll be careful, Maman," he said. "And I promise I'll be back as soon as I can." Then he set off in search of his father, who was still out there somewhere, alone and possibly stranded in the cold, dark night.

FOURTEEN

Marcel rode steadily along the main street until he reached the road that led out of town. This was the latest he had ever been out, and the truth was it made him a little scared. Oh, sure, he had acted brave in front of his mother. And he really did want to *be* brave. But cycling out here with the wind hissing through the trees and not a soul around was pretty scary.

A great, spotted bird with an enormous wingspan swooped down very low, startling him as it passed. It was so close he might have reached out to touch it. It flew away quickly but he thought he recognized the ear tufts and the big orange eyes of an eagle owl. It was probably hunting, on the lookout for a rabbit or mouse as its late-night supper, and he was relieved when it was gone.

To keep his spirits up, he pictured himself again in the Tour de France. Yesterday's ride was an exhausting stage of the race, but now he was on one of the last, crucial stages, pedaling toward the final finish line. Or what he hoped would be the final one.

The fantasy helped him push through his fear. Marcel pedaled on, slowing down when he came to the bridge. Sure enough, it was manned by a pair of gendarmes. One was short and tubby, the other, skinny and tall. He did not recognize either of them and his heart sped up as he got closer.

"You there," called the chubby one. "Come over here."

Marcel did as he was told.

"What are you doing out at this hour?" said the soldier. "You should be home in bed."

Marcel's heart was hammering. He did not want to say anything about looking for his father. If he did, the soldier might ask what *he* was doing out so late. And explaining that would put too many people he cared about at risk.

"I'm going to see my grandmother. She's alone and she needs me." Marcel's actual grandmother lived far away, in Lyon, so he did not think he was endangering her at all by saying this.

"Hmph," said the gendarme. "Still seems pretty late to me. You'd better turn around and go home."

Marcel remembered the tin he carried in his satchel and he dug inside to pull it out. "Here," he said. "I was bringing this to her, but you can have it. She really can't eat it anyway. She doesn't have too many teeth left." This wasn't true, either, but how would the soldier ever find out?

"Look at this," said the gendarme, opening the tin. *"Touron."* He took out a piece and ate it. "I haven't seen this in ages!"

"Don't eat it all!" said the taller of the two. "You'd better save some for me." He reached for the tin but his comrade held it out of reach.

"Stop being so greedy. You'll get yours," said the chubby one. "There's a whole tin of it here."

Marcel waited until the second solider was chewing contentedly before he dared to ask, "Excuse me, sir, but please can I go now? My grandmother is waiting . . ."

"Go on, get out of here," said the chubby one. "And you'd better stay over at your grandmother's house. I don't want to see you back here tonight, understand?"

"Yes, sir!" Marcel sped off, grateful to be free again. He kept going, alert to the subtle sounds of the night—any of them might signal his father. Soon he saw something big looming up ahead. What if it was a checkpoint, and there were gendarmes who would stop and question him? He had nothing to give them. Nothing!

Then something began to move, shifting and neighing in the dark. Could it be? As he got closer, he saw that it was Lulu, the speckled mare that pulled the bakery wagon. What a relief! He'd made it—he had ridden through that last, terrifying stage, in the dark and all alone. Now he'd crossed the finish line in his mind—and there, just beyond it, was his father!

Marcel pulled up close to the wagon and practically tossed the bicycle aside. "Papa!" he called, but softly, so as not to alert any soldiers who might have been passing through the area. "Papa, it's me!"

"Marcel!" Papa jumped up and brushed off his hands. "I can't believe you found me! How did you know to come looking?"

"I remembered the last time you had trouble with that wheel. I told Maman it might have happened again."

"You were right," Papa said. "I was so focused on getting your friend and her family out of town that I forgot about that pesky wheel. I didn't bring my tools with me and now I'm stuck."

"I brought your tools, Papa!" said Marcel. He shrugged his satchel from his shoulders, opened it, and dumped the tools onto the ground.

"Thank you, Marcel," Papa said. "Now I can fix it and we can be on our way home."

"How can you work in the dark?" Marcel asked.

"I have no choice," his father said. "A light might attract attention—of the wrong kind."

While Papa worked, Marcel asked about Delphine and her family.

"I brought them to the house in Saint-Girons. Tomorrow they'll head into the mountains and, if they're lucky, cross the border."

"Unless they get caught," said Marcel.

"Unless they get caught," said Papa. "But I think their chances are pretty good. The guide who's taking them is experienced. He'll do his best to keep them safe."

When Papa had finished fixing the wheel, Marcel told him about what the soldier had said. "We'd better hide you and this," his father said, hoisting the bicycle up and into the wagon. "Now you hop in, too."

Once Marcel had positioned himself next to the bicycle inside the wagon, his father covered him with the tarp and arranged the sacks of flour and grain around him. He was well hidden from view. Then Papa climbed up to the seat and gave the signal to Lulu. The wagon jolted slightly and they were off.

Marcel could not see anything as they rode, but he was aware of when the wagon stopped at the bridge, and some muffled words were exchanged between his father and the soldiers. He must have given them some of the bread that Maman had packed.

The wagon started moving, and Lulu kept up a steady, rhythmic pace. It was late, well past midnight, and Marcel was tired. He let his eyes close, and he drifted into sleep.

The next thing he knew, Papa was pulling back the tarp and helping him down from the wagon. Maman was awake and waiting for them when they came into the apartment, relieved that they were home. Then Marcel went straight to his room and sank into the deepest of sleeps.

In the morning, he still felt weary from all the activity of the night before. He went to school anyway, determined not to let his attention lapse. He didn't want his teacher singling him out again.

But Mademoiselle Babineaux seemed more interested in Delphine's empty seat than anything else. "Does anyone know where she is?" she asked. No one in the classroom raised a hand. Then she turned directly to Marcel. "Marcel, do you have any idea?"

Unable to look at her, he stared down at the top of his desk. "No, Mademoiselle Babineaux."

Marcel felt uncomfortable. He liked his teacher and had never lied outright to her before. And she had protected him yesterday. But what else could he do?

"Are you sure?" she asked.

"Yes, mademoiselle. I'm sure." There was a long moment when nothing was said. He waited for her to challenge or scold him. But it did not happen. She turned her attention to the lesson on arithmetic, and Marcel felt like he could breathe again.

It turned out that the subject of Delphine's absence was not closed, though. At recess, Thierry came swaggering up to him at the lunch table. "I don't believe what you told the teacher. Everyone knows you were friends with that Jew. And I bet you know where she's hiding."

"I-I do not," stammered Marcel, who just wanted to keep his distance.

"Liar! Liar!" Thierry began to chant. He was standing over Marcel, and his big, bulky body kept Marcel from standing up and leaving the table. Marcel was getting more and more nervous when all of a sudden, Guillaume and Arnaud came over.

"Leave him alone," Guillaume said.

"Why should I?" said Thierry. He turned to Marcel. "Jew lover," he taunted.

"He is not," said Arnaud. "At least no more than any of the rest of us. So he was friendly with her. Big deal."

"Big deal is right." Marcel was surprised at how strong and confident his own voice sounded. "She was the *best* cyclist around here," he added. "She beat all of us in a race and she knew more about cycling than anyone. More than me. And certainly more than *you*. She could have beaten you in her sleep." He looked up, no longer afraid, at Thierry. "So don't let me hear you talking about her anymore, understand?"

To his surprise, Thierry moved back a step or two. And then he turned and lumbered awkwardly back to his seat at a different table. "Jew lover," he muttered again. But he'd clearly been surprised by Marcel's new-found courage.

Arnaud and Guillaume sat down next to Marcel. "You're right about Delphine," said Guillaume. "That girl could really ride."

"She sure could," added Arnaud. Then he looked over at Thierry. "I don't think he's going to bother you anymore. He's just a big bully, and bullies can never stand a taste of their own medicine."

Marcel smiled. It was good to have his friends back on his side again. With Delphine gone, he'd been feeling really alone. He wondered for the tenth, twentieth, thirtieth time where and how she was. Did she and her family find another safe place to stay? Were the truck and chickens all gone? Where were they on their journey now? Had they been able to avoid getting caught? There was no way to know.

After school let out for the day, he did something he knew he was not supposed to do: He pedaled by the house where Delphine and her family had lived. He took care not to be seen, and he made it look like he was just riding around, not that he was there for any special reason.

He could see through the windows that the furniture and dishes were still there. Clothes and books, too. That made sense. Delphine and her parents had each taken only one small knapsack, no more than that. But seeing the house, Marcel could almost imagine that they would walk back in and resume their lives again. Of course, he knew that wasn't going to happen. They were on their way to Spain now, trekking through the mountains, alert to every sound they heard, every shift in the leaves they saw.

Marcel hopped off his bike and wheeled it over to the bushes, where he hid it. He didn't want to draw any extra attention to himself. Then he began walking around, looking for something he could not name. The red bicycle was gone, sold. He already knew that. So what was he doing here? What did he hope to find?

Some distance from the house was a shed. The door was open and he stepped inside. Not much of interest in here: a basket of moldy-looking turnips, a banged-up pot, a rusty shovel. Just stuff no one wanted. It looked like it had been here for years and years.

But then his eye was caught by something that looked newer than everything else: a lumpy package wrapped in a fairly new sheet of newspaper. He picked it up and opened it. Inside was the shiny silver bell that had been attached to Delphine's red bike. He recognized the bell right away, since he had so admired and envied it. She must have left it for him to find! Then he turned to the wrinkled piece of newspaper and smoothed it out. It was a page from the sporting section about the famous Belgian cyclist Sylvère Maes. Maes had won the Tour in 1939 and even though the race had been canceled this year, the article talked about what he was doing now to stay in shape and what his future racing plans looked like. Of course that was what Delphine would have chosen to wrap the bell. It was perfect.

He rolled up the paper into a small tube and put it carefully into his satchel, along with the bell. He could only hope Delphine and her family were finding their way on the dangerous mountain path, and that there would be a safe place for them on the other side.

Marcel was just about to hop on the bike and head for home when he saw a ginger cat sitting by the stone step in front of the house. Was this Delphine's cat? Her coat was dirty, but he was pretty sure he recognized the darker orange stripes on her body, and her white front paws. "Here, kitty," he said, and to his surprise, she came right over and delicately sniffed the hand he extended. Then she looked at him with her big amber-colored eyes, and when he was close enough, allowed him to stroke her head.

"You're a good kitty, aren't you?" he asked. He had promised Delphine his family would take her cat. But he hadn't been able to keep his promise then, and he couldn't do it now because he couldn't ride home with a squirming cat in his arms. He set her down and got back on his bike.

His mother fried a small fish for dinner, and afterward, Marcel walked back to Delphine's house with a bit of the skin wrapped in brown paper. He set it out on the ground and waited. Sure enough, the cat came over, and when she had finished eating, he scooped her up. She squirmed a bit, but he held on tight and would not let go until he'd carried her safely home.

FIFTEEN

Marcel showed the silver bell to his parents. "That was very thoughtful of her," said his mother.

"She knew it would be useful to you and she wanted you to have it," added his father.

Using one of Papa's screwdrivers and a pair of screws from the toolbox, Marcel attached the bell to the beat-up old bike he was now using. He still missed the bike he'd traded away, but he wasn't sorry he'd let it go. Not a bit. It was worth it.

And then a few weeks later, at Christmas, Papa and Maman surprised him with a new bicycle. Well, it wasn't new—money was very tight and they could not have afforded a brand-new one. But its bottle-green frame was in pretty good shape, and the seat, which had only a few marks on it, was made of real leather.

"Thank you, thank you, thank you!" Marcel cried as he wheeled it around the room.

"Careful you don't knock anything over!" Maman said. She moved aside the three wooden shoes that they had set out Christmas Eve for Père Noël to fill.

"I want to ride it right now!" he said.

"Don't worry, you'll have a chance to ride it soon enough," said Maman. And then she fixed them crêpes filled with the remains of a jar of preserves she'd been hoarding. They tasted so good. After they ate, they all went off to hear Mass at church. It was only later in the day that Marcel was able to ride, and the first thing he did was to pedal over to Arnaud's house to show off his gift.

"That is some bike you've got there!" Arnaud said. "It sure beats that old wreck you've been riding."

"It sure does," Marcel agreed happily. "And it's going to beat you, too, when we start racing again—you wait and see!"

"Don't count on it," said Arnaud. "In case you've forgotten, I'm still pretty fast."

"But neither of us are as fast as Delphine," Marcel said, his high spirits suddenly evaporating.

"No, we're not," agreed Arnaud. There was a silence, but it was not uncomfortable. Then Arnaud asked, "Did you ever find out what happened to her? I mean, she just . . . disappeared. We never saw her again."

"No, we didn't," said Marcel, and technically this was the truth. But even if it hadn't been, he would have maintained the fiction. He couldn't risk revealing the real story to his friend—even now.

Later, back at home, Marcel asked his father if he knew anything about what had happened to Delphine's family.

"I didn't hear that they were caught," said his father.

"So that means they got to Spain? And that they're all right?"

His father shook his head. "I wish I could tell you that was true, but in all honesty, I can't. I only know I didn't hear about anything *bad* happening to them. So that makes it easier to believe that nothing bad did."

Marcel understood. He just wasn't going to get a better answer than that—he'd simply have to live with not knowing. "At least we tried," he said to his father. "At least we tried as hard as we could."

"We certainly did," said his father. "Especially you, Marcel." Papa put his hand on his shoulder, just like he would have with one of his friends, or another man. Marcel felt good knowing that they had tried as hard as they did. And basking in the warm glow of his father's pride felt good, too.

January and February were long, cold months, with a lot more snow and ice than usual. Marcel wasn't able to ride the new green bike as much as he would have liked. Still, he continued to carry messages for his parents in loaves of bread. Even though Delphine and her family had gone, the work of the Resistance went on.

Then there was a day in early March that was surprisingly mild, with temperatures hovering around ten degrees Celsius. Sitting at his desk in school, Marcel couldn't help looking at the window to where he could hear a flock of birds twittering in the branches of a nearby tree. What a nice sound. After school he would take his bicycle out for a spin. It was warm enough.

As soon as the bell rang, he picked up his satchel and headed out of the building. He passed Thierry, but the bigger boy just scowled and let him pass without a word. Ever since their exchange back in December, Thierry hadn't bothered him. Maybe Guillaume was right: All it took to scare a bully was to give him a taste of his own medicine.

Walking down his street, he waved to his parents, who were both busy behind the counter of the bakery. He then hurried up the stairs, where he dropped his bag. He was hungry, but he was even more eager to get on the bike. He'd eat later, he decided, and went downstairs to hop on.

What a feeling! That first ride after a break felt so good, so thrilling. And Marcel knew that February and March were crucial early-season training periods for the Tour de France riders. These were the months when the cyclists rode long hours to accumulate as many kilometers in their legs as possible to gear up for the big racing season.

He sped along at a good pace, enjoying the feel of the almost-spring air that filled his lungs. The new bike handled very well, and soon he was out of town. The days were getting longer, just a few brief minutes a day, but the afternoons no longer seemed to end so abruptly with that heavy curtain of black that fell at four o' clock. Marcel rode and rode, pumping his legs, pushing hard on the pedals. The sun on his face made his mood even better.

Maybe soon the war would end and the Occupation would be over. The Tour de France would return to France and fill the roads with agile cyclists and adoring fans. Maybe Delphine would even come back and they would watch it together, cheering at the sidelines for their favorite athletes. But he didn't even know what had happened to her.

Marcel was not paying attention to how far he'd ridden and was surprised when he realized he'd reached the little village where he'd gotten a flat and traded his bike for that old wreck. Papa had ended up selling it for the parts—the bike itself was pretty useless.

As he passed through the town square he slowed down. There was a fountain, now dry, and a street of shops. Two German soldiers stood on the corner, and as Marcel rode by, they were joined by a third. He turned away, toward the bistro on the other side of the square. There was a lone French gendarme at one table, and a couple of old men at another, each immersed in a news-paper. One of them smoked a pipe and the smell of the smoke floated through the air. And then, to his utter surprise, Marcel saw the boy with whom he'd traded bikes. His hair was shorter now and he was a bit taller, but Marcel recognized him in an instant. The boy was even riding Marcel's old bike—he recognized that, too. When the boy caught sight of him, he came right over.

"*Salut*," he said. *Hello*.

"*Salut*," replied Marcel.

"That's a great-looking bike," said the boy. "Is it new?"

"It was a Christmas present," Marcel said. "From my parents."

The boy looked it over appreciatively. "What happened to the one you got from me?"

"My father ended up selling it," said Marcel, looking at his old bike. "How is that one? Do you still like it?"

"It's terrific," said the boy. "It handles really well. You were right: It was a great deal."

For me, too, thought Marcel. But he did not say this aloud.

"By the way," said the boy. "Did you make it to your aunt's house that night? Was your cousin all right?"

"Yes," said Marcel. "And she's fine now."

Marcel was uncomfortable at having to tell yet another lie to the boy. But it kept Delphine and her family safe. How he wished he knew if she still was safe!

He said good-bye to the boy and got back on his bike.

It was just getting dark and the air had cooled down considerably by the time he got home. It was only March, after all. Winter was not over. He mounted the stairs quickly in search of a snack—he was starved. There wasn't much to tempt him, though: some stale bread and an apple that had gone soft, but he sat down at the table to eat anyway.

Then he saw it. The letter, propped up against the earthenware bowl. It was addressed to him. Mail? Now, *that* was something that didn't happen too often. Almost never, in fact. Marcel picked it up to look more closely. There was no return address, but the postmark and the stamps indicated it was from Portugal. Portugal! That was near Spain, where Delphine and her family had been headed. Could it be . . . ?

Ignoring his bread and mushy apple, he tore open the envelope. Inside, there was no letter and no note, only a brightly colored sheet of paper, folded into thirds. When he opened it, he saw it was a page torn from a magazine or a catalog of some kind. It showed a smiling girl riding a shiny red bicycle. Strapped to the front of the bicycle was a wicker basket, and inside the basket was a tabby cat.

Marcel looked more closely at the girl. She had blonde curls and blue eyes. Delphine's hair was black but her eyes were blue. And like the girl in the picture, she had a cat, the ginger kitty that now kept the bakery mouse-free. It was Delphine who had sent this to him. It all fit. The girl, the bike, and the cat. She was sending a message, a message to say she had escaped—and that she was all right. He was as sure of it as he was of his own name.

Relief washed over him like a wave. And mixed in with the relief was admiration: How clever she was to have found this way to communicate. No one else in the whole world would have understood the meaning of this picture. No one but Marcel.

He refolded the page and slipped it back into the envelope before heading downstairs. The bakery was busy, so this wasn't the moment to show Maman and Papa the good news he'd gotten. He would tell them later, when the three of them were alone. He knew that they would be as filled with happiness as he was at this moment. He wondered whether he'd ever see Delphine again. He hoped so. But even if he didn't, he knew he would never forget her.

BRIEF HISTORY OF WORLD WAR II

World War II officially began in Europe on September 1, 1939, when German troops invaded Poland. Germany was led by Adolf Hitler, who was also the head of the Nazi party. Under Hitler's leadership, the Nazis were intent on destroying groups they saw as inferior, mainly the Jewish people, as well as many other minorities. Great Britain and France responded to this attack on Poland by declaring war on Germany on September 3. Soon other countries joined in. The war was fought between the Axis Powers (the main powers being Germany, Italy, and Japan) and the Allied Powers (the main powers being Britain, the Soviet Union, and France). The United States resisted getting involved in the war, but when the Japanese bombed the U.S. naval base at Pearl Harbor in Hawaii on December 7, 1941, America joined the war effort along with the Allied Powers.

The fighting spread throughout the world. Most battles took place in Europe, Southeast Asia, and the

Pacific Ocean. It was the deadliest war in all of human history—around 70 million people were killed and many were wounded.

The war in Europe ended with Germany's surrender on May 7, 1945. The war in the Pacific ended when Japan surrendered on September 2, 1945.

Time Line of World War II in France

1940

May 10   Germany invades France

June 14   German army marches into Paris

June 16   Premier of the French government resigns; Maréchal Pétain becomes premier of the Vichy government, which cooperated fully with the Germans (he is given full powers as chief of state on July 10)

June 22   France is divided into two zones: the Occupied Zone in the north and the Free Zone in the south

June 23   Hitler visits Paris

October 3   Jews are barred from public office and key professions, and are banned from theaters, cafés, restaurants, concerts, stores, swimming pools, parks, etc.

October 4	Foreign Jews are threatened with internment

1941

May 14	First roundup of Jews in Paris takes place
July 22	Jewish property begins to be confiscated
August 20	Drancy, a French internment camp, is officially opened
October 2–3	Seven synagogues are blown up in Paris

1942

January 20	German government works out the Final Solution in Berlin. This is a code name for the extermination of Europe's Jewish population.

June 1	Jews are required to wear a yellow armband with the Star of David and the word *Juif* written on it
June 22	Jews imprisoned at Drancy are shipped to the concentration camp Auschwitz for extermination
July 16–17	Massive roundup of Jews in Paris. These Jews were slated for deportation to concentration camps.

1943

Jews rounded up in the cities of southern France

1944

July 31	Last trainload of Jews leaves Drancy for Auschwitz
August 25–26	Paris is liberated

SHORT HISTORY OF THE TOUR DE FRANCE

Did you know that the Tour de France was originally started in 1903 as a newspaper stunt? Desperate to improve the circulation of his ailing daily sports paper, *L'Auto*, journalist Géo Lefèvre came up with the idea of sponsoring a grand-scale bicycle race. Helping him was Henri Desgrange, the director-editor of *L'Auto* and a former champion cyclist himself.

Together, the two men developed a 1,500-mile clockwise loop of the country that ran from Paris to Lyon, Marseille, Toulouse, Bordeaux, and Nantes, and finally back to Paris. There were six stages (today there are thirteen) and no Alpine climbs. But the distances covered were, on average, a punishing 250 miles each. (Today, no single stage is more than 150 miles). Riders took between one and three days to recover between each stage. The length of time each rider took to complete each stage was added together. The rider with the lowest number overall was the winner.

On July 1, 1903, sixty men mounted their bicycles outside the Café au Reveil Matin in Montgeron, a suburb of Paris. The riders were mostly French, with a few Belgians, Swiss, Germans, and Italians thrown into the mix. Bicycle manufacturers sponsored about twenty or so professionals. The others were men who just loved the sport. Each rider wanted to prove that he was the best cyclist. And they all wanted to win the 20,000 francs offered in prize money.

The first race began at 3:16 p.m. The first stage, a 300-mile stretch from Paris to Lyon, was especially hard. Cyclists in 1903 rode over unpaved roads without helmets. They could receive no help and they could not glide in the slipstream of fellow riders or any other vehicles. Cyclists had to make their own repairs. They even rode with spare tires and tubes wrapped around their torsos in case they got flats along the way.

Unlike today's riders, the cyclists in the 1903 Tour de France also rode by night, with only the moon and stars to guide them. Many riders could not tolerate this. All in all, twenty-three riders abandoned the first stage of the race.

The leader of the remaining pack was a thirty-two-year-old Frenchman named Maurice Garin. As a teenager, he had worked as a chimney sweep and later became one of France's best cyclists. A little more than seventeen hours after the start of the race outside Paris, Garin, covered in mud, crossed the finish line of the first stage in Lyon. He had won by a single minute.

As the race went on, Garin continued to gain ground. By the fifth stage, he was ahead by two hours. When his nearest competitor was slowed down by two flat tires *and* because he fell asleep while resting on the side of the road, Garin pulled sharply ahead. The sixth and final stage, which was the longest, began in Nantes at 9:00 p.m. on July 18. Fans lined up to watch the riders arrive in Paris late the following afternoon. Garin strapped on a green armband to signify his position as race leader. (The yellow jersey worn by the race leader was not introduced until 1919.)

Twenty thousand fans poured into the Parc des Princes velodrome to cheer as Garin won both the stage and the first Tour de France. He was almost three hours ahead of his nearest competitor, Lucien Pothier. In total, Garin had been riding for more than ninety-five hours. His average speed was 15 miles per hour. When the race was over, only twenty-one of the sixty riders who entered completed the Tour. The last-place rider came in sixty-four hours after Garin.

Desgrange's big gamble had paid off. Newspaper circulation soared during the race and a new tradition was born. Today, more than 110 years later, the Tour de France continues to be wildly popular with cycling fans all over the world. Boys and girls like Marcel and Delphine continue to idolize the cyclists' remarkable athletic gifts and their fierce determination to win. Here are some fun facts about how the big race has evolved over time:

- At first, Desgrange did not allow the use of multiple gears on the bicycles, and for many years insisted riders use bicycles with wooden rims, because he was afraid the heat of braking while coming down mountains would melt the glue that held the tires on metal rims. Metal rims were finally allowed in 1937.

- In 1903, Desgrange had allowed riders who dropped out one day to continue the next for daily prizes but not the overall prize. In 1928, he allowed teams who had lost members to replace them halfway through the race.

- Night riding was dropped after the second Tour in 1904. Riding in the dark made it just too easy to cheat.

- Endurance was always a key element. Desgrange said his ideal race would be so hard that only one rider would make it to Paris.

- The first three Tours stayed within France and ran around the perimeter of the country. Over the years, the cycling route expanded, and now Belgium, Britain, Germany, Italy, Spain, and Switzerland are part of the race. More difficult mountain routes, through the Pyrenees and the Alps, were also added.

- Henri Desgrange planned a Tour for 1940, after the war had started but before France had been invaded. Then the Germans invaded and the race was not held again until 1947.

- From 1984 to 1989, a women's stage race was held, and in 2014, the last men's stage was preceded by a women's race, called La Course. It was won by Marianne Vos.

- The Tour de France has always offered a big prize. In addition to money, prizes have also included cars, apartments, and artwork. In 1990, the prizes went back to being cash.

- Four riders have won five times: Jacques Anquetil (France), Eddy Merckx (Belgium), Bernard Hinault (France), and Miguel Indurain (Spain). Indurain is the only rider to have won five consecutive times, from 1991 to 1995.

GLOSSARY OF TERMS

Baguette—A long, thin loaf of bread, traditional in France. The word *baguette* means *wand* in French.

Cassoulet—A French stew made of beans, herbs, sausage, and sometimes other meats, and simmered for several hours.

Collaborator—Term used by the French to describe the people who went along with the Germans, obeyed their orders, and carried out their plans.

Concentration camps—Camps where inmates were imprisoned and used as slave labor or, in many cases, murdered outright. Jews, Sinti and Roma, Communists, and homosexuals were just some of the people sent to the camps.

Cornichons—Small, hard, and very sharp-tasting, these tiny green pickles are commonly served in France.

Croissant—A flakey, crescent-shaped French pastry, often served for breakfast with butter and jam.

Free Zone—The southern part of France that was not initially occupied by the military, although by 1942, the Germans occupied the entire country.

Gendarme—A soldier, especially in France, serving in an army group acting as armed police with authority over civilians.

Gestapo—The official secret police of Nazi Germany and German-occupied Europe. One of the Gestapo's chief jobs was to hunt down and capture Jews.

***Merci**—Thank you* in French.

***Mon Dieu!**—My God!* in French.

Nazi Party—Started in 1920 and led by Adolf Hitler, the National Socialist German Workers' Party (Nazi for short) believed that Germans, especially those with blond hair and blue eyes, were a master race and deserved to dominate all other people.

Occupied Zone—The northern part of France that was taken over when the German army invaded the country in 1940.

***Pain d'épice**—Literally, spice bread* in French. The French version of gingerbread.

Ration cards—Because food, fuel, and other essentials were all being used for the war effort, there were many shortages. People were issued cards by the government that allowed them to buy a limited amount of any given item. This way, no one could buy too much and try to resell these items at a higher price.

Resistance—A loosely formed underground movement of French citizens who opposed the Germans and worked secretly to overthrow them. When they could, Resistance members helped by hiding Jews or leading them safely out of France.

Swastika—A 5,000-year-old religious symbol common in ancient Greece, for example, and still found today in India and Indonesia. Adolf Hitler adopted it as the symbol of the Nazi party.

Touron—A sweet candy that is filled with nuts and dried fruit. It is a specialty of southwest France.

Vichy government—Vichy was the temporary French government set up in unoccupied France in 1940. The Vichy regime was fully cooperative with the invading Germans.

Zut and *zut alors*—French for *heck* or *darn*.

For Further Reading

- *DK Eyewitness World War II*, Simon Adams and Andy Crawford, DK Publishing, 2000

- *History Hits: Second World War: The Fun Bits of History You Don't Know About*, Callum Evans, Thought Junction Publishing, 2015

- *The Doll with the Yellow Star*, Yona Zeldis McDonough, Henry Holt, 2005

About the Author

Yona Zeldis McDonough is the award-winning author of twenty-seven books for children and seven novels for adults. Her essays, articles, and short fiction have appeared in numerous national and literary publications. She is also the fiction editor of *Lilith* magazine. McDonough lives in Brooklyn with her husband and their two children.